May 2, 1995

Don Rodrigo,

I FOUND A COPY OF THIS LITTLE BRITISH
BOOK MY FIRST SEMESTER AT GW - WHEN I
WAS ALSO TEACHING MY FIRST INTRO COURSE.
I MISTAKENLY THOUGHT THE TITLE WAS "THE
EVOLUTION OF MAN". IT ISN'T - BUT IT TURNED
OUT TO BE EVEN MORE WONDEROUS. I HOPE
YOU'LL ENJOY IT DURING YOUR WELL-DESERVED
SABBATICAL.

HAPPY BIRTHDAY AND LOVE, BOB & JOHANNA

THE
EVOLUTION MAN
OR
HOW I ATE MY FATHER

THE
EVOLUTION MAN
OR
HOW I ATE MY FATHER

ROY LEWIS

PANTHEON BOOKS NEW YORK

All rights reserved under International and
PanAmerican Copyright Conventions.
Published in the United States by Pantheon Books,
a division of Random House, Inc., New York,
and simultaneously in Canada by Random House
of Canada Limited, Toronto. Originally published in
Great Britain as *What We Did to Father* by Hutchinson,
an imprint of Century Hutchinson Publishing Ltd.,
London, in 1960.

Library of Congress
Cataloging-in-Publication Data

Lewis, Roy, 1913–
[What we did to father]
The evolution man, or,
How I ate my father / Roy Lewis.
p.   cm.
Originally published: What we did to father.
London : Hutchinson, 1960.
ISBN 0-679-42727-9
1. Man,   Prehistoric—Fiction.   I. Title.
II. Title: How I ate my father.
PR6062.E9538W47   1993
823′.914—dc20   93-3359
CIP

Book Design by M. Kristen Bearse

Manufactured in the United States of America

First American Edition

9   8   7   6   5   4   3   2   1

To my darling daughters,
Dr. Theodore Reik,
and some others

THE
EVOLUTION MAN
OR
HOW I ATE MY FATHER

CHAPTER 1

When the winds blew strongly from the North, bringing an icy reminder that the great ice-cap was still advancing, we used to pile all our stores of brushwood and broken trees in front of the cave, make a really roaring fire, and tell ourselves that however far south it came this time, even in Africa, we could meet it and beat it.

We were often hard put to it to keep up the supply of fuel for a big fire, even though a good edge on quartzite will cut through a four-inch bough of cedar in ten minutes; it was the elephants and mammoths who kept us warm with their thoughtful habit of tear-ing up trees to test the strength of their tusks and trunks. *Elephas antiquus* was even more given to this than is the modern type, for he was still hard at it evolving, and there is nothing that an evolving animal worries about more than how his teeth are getting along. The mammoths, who reckoned that they were just about perfect in those days, only tore up trees when they were angry or showing off to the females. In the mating season we had only to follow the herds to collect firewood, but at other times a well-aimed stone behind the ear of a browsing mammoth would work wonders, and maybe set you up in kindling for a month. I have known that gambit to work with the big mastodons, but an uprooted baobab takes a good deal of dragging home. They burn well, but keep you at a distance of a hundred feet. There is no sense in taking things to extremes. By and large, we kept a good fire going when it was chilly and the ice-caps on Kilimanjaro and the Ruwenzori descended under the 10,000-foot contour line.

The sparks flew up to the stars on cold clear wintry nights, the green wood hissed and the dry wood crackled, and our fire was quite a beacon all down the Rift Valley. When ground temperatures were low enough, or the dank rain closed in and made one's joints creak and ache, Uncle Vanya would come and visit us. During a lull in the noise of the jungle traffic you would hear him coming, with a swish-swish-swish through the tree-tops, punctuated by an occasional ominous crack of an overburdened branch, and a muffled oath, which became a scream of uninhibited rage when he actually fell.

At last he would shamble into the circle of firelight, a massive figure, his long arms practically trailing the ground, his square head crouched down between his broad, hairy shoulders, his eyes bloodshot, his lips curled back in the effort which he customarily made to get his canines to stick outside them. This gave him, as it happened, the expression of one who has put on a completely false smile at a party which he greatly dislikes; and as a small boy I found it absolutely terrifying. But later on I discovered behind all his fads and eccentricities—from which he was the first to suffer, and indeed the only one—a kindly person always ready with a tip of juniper berries or figs for a boy who he fondly supposed was properly taken in by the natural ferocity of his appearance.

But how he talked, how he argued! He barely saluted us, and nodded in Aunt Mildred's direction, barely held out his poor hands, blue with cold, to the blaze, before he got started, going for Father like a rhinoceros with its head down, his long, accusing forefinger pointing for all the world like the tip of its horn. Father would let him charge and work off his pent-up feelings in a torrent of denunciation; then when he had calmed down a little, and perhaps eaten a couple of aepyornis's eggs and a few durians, Father would join the fray, parrying Uncle Vanya's thrusts with his mild, ironic interjections, and at times reducing him to stupefied speechlessness by gaily admitting his enormities and taking positive credit for them.

I believe that at bottom they were deeply fond of one another though they had spent their whole lives in violent disagreement; this could hardly be otherwise since they were both ape-men of unswerving principle, who lived in strict accordance with their beliefs, and their principles were totally opposed at every point. Each went his own way, firmly convinced that the other was tragically mistaken about the direction in which the anthropoid species was evolving; but their personal relationship was, if uninhibited, also quite unimpaired. They argued, they even shouted at each other; but they never came to blows. And though Uncle Vanya usually left us in high dudgeon he always came back.

The first time that I can remember a set-to between the brothers, so utterly unlike in appearance and demeanour, was over the whole business of having a fire on cold nights at all. I was squatting well away from the red, writhing, wounded yet voracious thing, watching how Father fed it with a splendid if circumspect nonchalance. The women were huddled together, chattering as they deloused each other; my mother as always a little apart, staring at Father and the fire with her sombre brooding eyes as she masticated pap for the weaned babies. Then suddenly Uncle Vanya was among us, a menacing figure, speaking in a voice of doom.

"You've done it now, Edward," he rumbled. "I might have guessed this would happen sooner or later, but I suppose I thought there was a limit even to your folly. But of course I was wrong! I've only got to turn my back on you for an hour and I find you up to some fresh idiocy. *And now this!* Edward, if ever I warned you before, if ever I begged you, as your elder brother, to think again before you continued on your catastrophic course, to amend your life before it involved you and yours in irretrievable disaster, let me now say, with tenfold emphasis: Stop! Stop, Edward, before it is too late—if indeed you still have time, stop . . ."

Uncle Vanya drew breath before he completed this impressive but obviously difficult period to round off, and Father chipped in.

"Why, Vanya, we certainly haven't seen you for quite a while. Come and get warm, my dear chap. Where have you been?"

Uncle Vanya made an impatient gesture.

"Not all that far. It's been rather a poor season for the fruit and vegetables on which I rely rather heavily for my diet—"

"I know," said Father in a sympathetic voice. "Looks like we may be in for an interpluvial after all. I've noticed the way desiccation is spreading lately."

"But not exclusively, by any means," went on Uncle Vanya irritably. "There's plenty to eat in the forest if you know where to look. I happen to find that I have to be careful just what I eat at my time of life—so, like any sensible primate, I went a little farther afield to find what I wanted—to the Congo, in fact, where there is plenty of everything for everybody, without having to pretend that you have the teeth of a leopard, the stomach of a goat or the taste and manners of a jackal, Edward!"

"That's putting it rather strongly, Vanya," protested Father.

"I came back yesterday," went on Uncle Vanya, "intending to pay you a visit in any case. Of course at nightfall I knew something was wrong. Eleven volcanoes on this district I know of, Edward—but twelve! I knew there was trouble afoot, and I half knew you were at the bottom of it. Hoping against hope, but dread in my heart, I hurried here. How right I was. Private volcanoes indeed! you've done it now, Edward!"

Father grinned mischievously. "Do you really think so, Vanya?" he asked. "I mean, is this really the turning point? I thought it might be, but it's hard to be quite sure. Certainly *a* turning point in the ascent of man, but is it *the*?" Father wrinkled up his eyes in a look of humorous desperation that was characteristic of him at certain moments.

"I don't know whether it's a turning point or the turning point," said Uncle Vanya. "I don't profess to know what you think you are doing, Edward. Getting above yourself, yes. I'm telling you that this is the most perverse and unnatural—"

"It is unnatural, isn't it?" said Father, eagerly breaking in. "But then, Vanya, there has been an element of the artificial in subhuman life since we took to stone tools. Perhaps, you know, that was the *decisive* step, and this is simply elaboration; but then *you* use flints and so—"

"We've had that out before," said Uncle Vanya. "Within reason tools and artifacts do not transgress nature. The spiders take their prey by net; the birds can build better nests then we can; and many's the time you have had a coconut thrown at your thick head by a monkey, as you well know; perhaps that is what has deranged your wits. Only a few weeks ago I saw a troop of gorillas beat up a couple of elephants —elephants, mark you!—with sticks. I am prepared to accept simple trimmed pebbles as in the way of nature, provided one does not become too dependent on them, and no attempt is made to refine them unduly. I am not illiberal, Edward, and I will go as far as that. But *this*! This is quite another matter. This could end anywhere. It affects everybody. Even me. You might burn the forest down with it. Then where would I be?"

"Oh, I don't think it will come to that, Vanya," said Father.

"Won't it, indeed! May I ask, Edward, are you in control of the thing at all?"

"Er—more or less. More or less, you know."

"What do you mean, more or less? Either you are, or you are not. Don't prevaricate. Can you put it out, for example?"

"If you don't feed it, it goes out of itself," said Father defensively.

"Edward," said Uncle Vanya, "I warn you. You have started something that you may not be able to stop. So you think it will go out if you don't feed it! Have you thought that it might decide to feed itself, sometime? Then where would you be?"

"It hasn't happened yet," said Father crossly. "It takes me all my time to keep it going, as a matter of fact, especially on wet nights."

"Then my most earnest advice to you is not to keep it going any longer," said Uncle Vanya, "before you get a chain reaction started. How long have you been playing with fire?"

"Oh, I found out about it months ago," said Father. "And, you know, Vanya, it is the most fascinating stuff. The possibilities are stupendous. I mean, there is so much you can do with it. Far beyond mere central heating, you know, though that's a big step forward in itself. I have hardly begun to work out the applications yet. But just take the smoke alone: believe it or not, it smothers the flies and keeps down the mosquitoes. Of course, fire is tricky stuff. Hard to carry about, for instance. Then it's got a voracious appetite; eats like a horse. Apt to be spiteful, got a nasty sting, if you're not careful. And it really is new; opens up a positive vista of—"

But suddenly there was a loud shriek from Uncle Vanya and he began hopping about on one foot. I had observed with great interest that for some time he had been standing on a red-hot ember. He had been too excited in his argument with Father to notice it, or the hissing noise and peculiar smell which followed. But now the ember had bitten right through the hide of his instep.

"Yah!" roared Uncle Vanya. "You damned fool, Edward! It's bitten me! That's what your infernal bag of tricks has done! Yah! What did I tell you? It'll end by eating the whole lot of you! Sitting on a live volcano, that's what you're doing! I've finished with you, Edward! You'll be extinct, the whole pack of you, in no time. You've had it. Yah! I'm going back to the trees! You've overstepped the mark this time, Edward! That's what the brontosaurus did, too!"

He soon hobbled out of sight, but his howls could be heard for another fifteen minutes at least.

"All the same, I guess it was Vanya who overstepped the mark," said Father to Mother, as with a leafy branch he carefully swept the hearth.

CHAPTER 2

Uncle Vanya returned, notwithstanding, to repeat his warnings many times, especially on cold or rainy nights. His misgivings were not at all appeased by our gradual progress in fire-control. He snorted contemptuously when we showed him how to damp it down, how it could be cut up, like an eel, into several fires, and how it could be carried on the tip of dry branches. Even though all these experiments were carefully supervised by Father, Uncle Vanya condemned them; botany and zoology he considered to be the whole content of a scientific education, and he was entirely opposed to adding physics to the curriculum.

Yet we all took to it very quickly. The women were at first slow to get out of the way and burned themselves; and for a time it looked as if the youngest generation would not survive at all. But Father thought that everyone should make his own mistakes. "A burned child respects the fire," he would say confidently as yet another baby began screeching after it had grabbed a fiery beetle. He was right.

These were, after all, small accidents to set against the gain. Our standard of living rose almost out of recognition. Before we had fire, we were in a very small way. We had come down from the trees, we had the stone axe; but we had not much more, and every tooth and claw and horn in nature seemed to be against us. Though we considered ourselves as ground animals, we had to nip up a tree pretty smartly again if we got into any sort of a jam. We still had to live on berries, roots and nuts to a great extent, we were still glad of fat caterpillars and grubs to strengthen the intake of protein. Of energy-giving foods we were chronically short, though we needed them desperately to sustain our growing physique. One important reason for leaving the forest was to get more meat into our diet. There was plenty of meat on the plains; the trouble was, it was all on four legs. The great grasslands were crowded with game: great herds of bison, buffalo, impala, oryx, wildebeeste, hartebeeste, antelope, gazelle, zebra and horse, to mention only a few of those we would have liked to dine on. But chasing meat on four legs when you are trying to go about on two is a mug's game; and we were forced to try and stand up in order to see over the top of the savannah grass. Even if you caught a big ungulate, what could you do with it? It kicked you. Sometimes you could run a lame animal down; then it presented its horns to you. A horde of ape-men was needed to stone it to death. With a horde, you can surround and run down game; but to keep a horde together needs a large and regular food supply. This is the oldest of vicious circles in economics: to make any sort of bag you need a team of hunters; but to feed a team you must be sure of a regular bag. Otherwise mealtimes are so irregular that you can feed a little group of three or four at best.

We had therefore to start right at the bottom and work our way up. We had to begin with rabbits, hyrax and minor rodents which you can knock over with a stone; we had to go after turtles and tortoises, lizards and snakes, which can be caught if you study their habits with assiduity. Once killed, small ground game can be cut up with flint knives fairly handily, and though the best part of the meat is not easy to tear and eat without the big canines of the carnivores, it can be cut up and smashed a bit with stones prior to mastication by molars which were primarily designed for a frugivorous diet. The soft parts are often not very nice, but people who are hungry with the effort of walking upright all day on their hind legs, and who want to nourish their brains, cannot afford to be fastidious. We competed for the soft parts and set high store on mushy animals, because they relieved the strain on our teeth and digestions.

I doubt if many people remember today what agonies of indigestion we endured in those early times; or indeed how many succumbed to it. Tempers were permanently soured by gastric disturbances; and the lowering sullen grimace of the subhuman pioneers of primordial days had far less to do with their moroseness or savagery than the condition of their stomach linings. The sunniest disposition is apt to be undermined by chronic colitis. It is a complete fallacy to suppose that, because we were just down from the trees and to that extent "nearer to nature," we could eat just anything, however unpalatable or stringy it might be. On the contrary, to widen one's feeding habits from the purely vegetarian (and almost wholly frugivorous at that) towards omnivorousness is a painful and difficult process, demanding immense patience and persistence in discovering how to keep down things which not only disgust one, but disagree with one as well. Only unrelenting ambition, the desire to improve one's place in nature, and ruthless self-discipline will carry one through that transition. I am not denying that there are unexpected tidbits to be found, but life cannot be all snails and sweetbreads. Once you set out to be omnivorous you must learn to eat *everything*, and in times when you never know where the next meal is coming from you must also eat everything *up*. As children we were brought up most strictly on these rules; and a child who dared to say, "But, Mummy, I don't like toad!" was a child asking to have its ears boxed. "Eat it up; it's good for you," was the refrain of my childhood; and of course it is true—nature, marvellously adaptable, did somehow harden our little insides to digest the indigestible.

It must be remembered that in becoming meateaters we had to chew, and therefore to taste, all this rich, unsuitable food. The carnivores—the great cats, the wolves and dogs, the crocodiles—merely tore their meat into pieces and swallowed it, careless of whether it was shoulder, rump steak, liver or tripes.

We could not bolt our food. "Chew one hundred times before you swallow," another maxim of childhood, was based on the certainty that severe bellyache would follow if it was ignored. However nasty the gobbet, in primeval times it had to be well explored by the mouth and palate. Hunger was our only sauce; but that we had in plenty.

So we envied the huge banquets of meat which the lions and sabre-tooths struck down so casually and ate of so wastefully, leaving perhaps three-quarters of a carcass for the jackals and vultures. Our first concern was therefore whenever possible to be in at the lion's kill, and, when he had taken his share, to take the remainder. We were at least the equal of the jackal and the vulture, with our axes and our well-aimed stones and our pointed sticks, though we often had to fight hard. Our best meals often came by watching the vultures and racing them to the spot; though of course to be a scavenger carries the disadvantage that you have to keep in the vicinity of the killer, and most of all when he is hungry. This involves the risk that you will provide his dinner yourself.

It was a big risk. The jackal and hyaena can run; the vulture can fly; but your poor ape just down from the trees must walk warily in the plains. There were plenty who did not care for that dangerous life and confined themselves to small game, nasty as it often was, and to the small, unstimulating parochial society which was all it could support. The best-fed, biggest and most enterprising people were undoubtedly those who followed the big cats—lion, sabre-tooth, leopard, cheetah, lynx and the rest of the tribe—and dined when they left the table. It was dangerous work, but those who preferred its rewards always maintained that the cats would eat primate flesh anyway, if only for a change from their usual meat; by keeping close to them you did not greatly increase the risk of being hunted yourself, but on the other hand you learned a great deal that was useful about their habits which enabled you to take avoiding action at need. Then, when you *did* have to run for it, you were well-nourished and in good training. The great thing was to know when a lion was hungry and when he was not; casualties could be halved by careful observance of this one point alone. I have heard it objected that hunting with the lion is what gave the lion his taste for us; but those early hunters hotly denied it, as they also resented the slighting suggestion that they were mere parasites on the higher carnivores. It must be accepted, I think, that they did after all learn a very great deal about beasts of prey which will be of permanent use to humanity.

We might make something out of the carnivores, but we were no match for them. We did not dare to cross them. They were the lords of creation, and their will was law. They kept our numbers firmly down, and there was very little we could do about it, except go back to the trees and give the whole thing up as a bad job. As Father was absolutely convinced that we were on the right track, there was no question of that, except for people like Uncle Vanya. Father was serenely certain that something would turn up to re-store our fortunes; we had put our trust in intelli-gence, in a big brain and a big skull to keep it in, and we must trust to it to see us through somehow. Meantime, we must have as good a pair of legs as possible. "There is no earthly reason," I heard Father say more than once, "why an ape-man should not be able to run a hundred metres in ten seconds, jump over a seven-foot thornbush or, using a spear, vault a fifteen-and-a-half-foot one; given a decent start and biceps to swing oneself up from branch to branch, that should get you out of trouble ninety times in a hundred." I have seen him prove this himself.

This was all very well, but it did not solve the

major problem or settle the host of minor inconveniences which are inevitable when the cat tribe is the ruling class. One of these is undoubtedly housing. Every ape-woman wants a decent place in which to bring up her family, a real home, snug, warm and, above all, dry; nobody, I fancy, will deny that basically this means a cave. Nothing else really meets the problem of the prolongation of childhood, the steady extension of the educational process beyond the primary stage, which is the outstanding characteristic of our species. Up in the fork of a tree you are comparatively safe, but you have got to sleep sitting astride and hanging on, and everyone who has done it—and few of us, benighted upon our lawful occasions, even in these enlightened days, have not done it—knows how extremely uncomfortable it is. Even chimpanzees sometimes fall off if they have a nightmare—that dreadful falling feeling which, when you wake up, you find to be perfectly true. For a woman it is worse since she has to hang on to one or more children at the same time. This becomes more and more impossible as women give up growing their hair on their chests and as children lose their inherited prehensile reactions at a progressively early age.

Of course you can make a nest on the ground. Nesting is a widespread instinct; even if it were not, there are the birds to learn from. A very desirable little nest can be woven in a few hours from any suitable material, such as bamboo and palm fronds; and quite an imposing residence of boughs can be erected in a week if occupation is to be extended. In such a nest one can stretch one's limbs at night. But it does not turn a heavy shower of rain, and it does not turn even a light leopard. However carefully you cover it with leaves, however skilfully you conceal it in the bushes, when things are difficult you tend to get rheumatism and to lose Junior.

Every ape-woman wants a cave, even quite a little cave, with a roof over her head, solid rock at her back, and a narrow opening in which she can stand at bay for her whelps with some chance of success. She can then bar the door with an uprooted tree, and she may even have a niche high up inside where she can cache Baby or which she can use as a larder. But of course animals know all this as well as we do, the bears as well as the lions or sabre-tooths, and there are never enough caves to go round. There are few that could not be filled over and over again with homeless families of every kind. But nobody will share, except perhaps snakes. We found that if one of the big cats occupied a cave, you had to let him keep it as a rule; and if you had it, and he wanted it, as a rule you had to pack up and go. But that did not stop the women from complaining about it.

Not at all. They went on and on and on about it. Half their conversation was about caves; lovely little caves that they had *had*—until their males allowed a big brute of a bear to turn them out of it; wonderfully dry roomy caves in the next district which could be *got*, if one had any real feeling for a woman's point of view, merely by moving a quite *small* pride of lions a few miles farther on (where there were plenty more caves anyway); perfect caves that could be *found*, without any lions in them at all, if one only looked round a bit instead of making excuses about the need to chip flints all day; and the uselessness of the wretched cave which they actually *had*—which was not a cave worthy of the name, but a mere rock-shelter, a bit of cliff with a slight overhang, which the rain blew into, and just listen to Baby's *dreadful* cough.

It is true enough that we were often cold and wet as well as hungry at night, and frightened too, as the darkness was rent by the grunt-grunt of the lion putting up game, or the baying of packs of dogs on the scent. You would listen and hear the enemy coming nearer and nearer, as you crouched together against your miserable bit of rock—down which, of course, an icy rivulet would always and inexplicably start to flow—the women holding the children, the males grasping their hand-axes or sticks, even the boys gripping a stone to throw. Nearer the hunt would come and nearer; then there would come the shriek of some stricken deer, and you would know that it wasn't your turn yet. Then an hour or two of fitful sleep and the hunt was up again. Bright eyes glared at the little horde from the dark line of the jungle—gleamed and passed on or drew nearer to the poor thin frieze of pointed sticks that defended our lair and gave us perhaps an extra second or two in which to hurl the rock or stab with the stick. Then down on us like a great projectile would crash the huge body, eyes blazing, jaws agape, snarl rising to its crescendo of triumph; we would rise with our yell of defiance and then all was mêlée—sticks whirling, stones flying, jaws snapping and razor-tipped paws flashing out and ripping at bare thighs and exposed bellies. And then the raider would be gone, leaving us battered and bleeding—and somebody small would be missing.

So much for intelligence versus striped muscle and retractable claws! We sometimes won even against a direct frontal attack. Sometimes we were ensconced on a ledge just out of reach (and proportionately uncomfortable) and developed our vocabulary of insult in the angry face of the battled attacker. Sometimes a well-aimed rock sent the big bully off with a big headache. Once, I remember, we killed, and promptly ate, a marauding sabre-tooth; he had lost his sabres on somebody else and thought we were easier meat. But my strongest memories are of the long nights of waiting in an exposed position, poorly fortified; of the growing roars of the enemy, the gleaming eyes, the charge.

There was nothing you could do but wait and listen, your mouth dry, your stomach hollow, your heart thumping, your knees flexed for action. Long sleepless nights we made of it in the worst seasons, when we seemed to be hunted by packs of carnivores taking us in turn. The men dwindled, killed outright or dead of wounds; mere boys stood in the front line. And still they came. And then, one night, Father was not there either. That morning he had surveyed the scene of carnage left after the previous night's battle. His face was grey with weariness, lined with sorrow. Then he had turned and loped off into the forest saying, merely: "Back tonight. Got to do something important." My mother had sighed heavily, and continued to bind up with leaves and one of the sloughed snake-skins she kept for such emergencies, a horrible gash in my brother's shoulder. She had lost Pepita, my youngest sister, that night. But when darkness fell again, Father had not returned. Always at nightfall he had supervised the rebuilding and strengthening of the stockade, had insisted that everyone should have something to eat, if it was only roots and berries, had inspected the axes and sharpened the spears. We knew what his absence meant—an argument with a mammoth, a foot placed incautiously on a crocodile —and wearily prepared to do as he had always bid us. At last a sickle moon began to rise among the stars and we knew it was going to be bad again.

They came and glared with those burning eyes; prowled round and went on; and told the moon that they were hungry and must eat; and went and hunted; and returned to us again. Some unknown one-eyed beast I saw coming from far away; half-asleep and half-awake I saw it inside my head as a huge lizard with a volcano burning on its forehead as it moved relentlessly towards us, a vast armour-plated leviathan which would swallow us up in the friendliest manner, making an end of this insupport-able ordeal. On it came, treading lesser creatures into the ground, nearer, larger and brighter, determined to get to us before the lions and leopards selected the choicest morsels, or the wolves swept down ravenous and overwhelming. And just as all the teeth in the jungle seemed to converge on our stockade, suddenly the strange beast sprang, small and lithe and brown and biped, into our midst, and tore a red hole in the blackness of the night. And it was Father, holding his hand aloft; and in his hand, captive in a stick, flaring and smoking with menace, thrusting back the jungle far beyond the lion's leap, was fire.

CHAPTER 3

The next morning Father led us forth, a small bedraggled procession, from that blood-spattered ledge to the finest cave in the district. It had a fine arched portico, perhaps fifteen feet wide and twenty high, protected by a graciously weathered rocky overhang from which sprays of bougainvillaea hung to provide a curtain. In front of it a wide, smooth platform of rock served at once as hearth and loggia with a pleasant sunward aspect; it was flanked by a grove of cedar through which ran a constant cold water supply, adequate for drinking, bathing and sewage disposal. Within, the cave was commodious: the central hall was upwards of thirty-five feet deep and not quite so broad, with a vaulted roof. From this at both sides were recessed a number of inner caves and alcoves; while at the end a narrow tunnel led into the very bowels of the hills. Both my father and mother surveyed these modern conveniences with the utmost satisfaction.

"At last the girls will get a bit of privacy," said Mother.

"Vaults," said Father, peering into the tunnel. "Scope for development. Bats, of course; but we'll soon clear them out. Smelly, but perfectly nutritious. An inner sanctum, a—er—wine cellar one of these days, who knows?"

"And plenty of space in front for the kitchen-midden," said Mother.

"Yes, my dear," Father agreed. "I think it will suit us very well."

The cave had long been the home of a large family of bears, who stared at us with utter amazement as we marched upon them to throw them out. They could hardly believe their eyes. It must have looked as if dinner was being served. Then suddenly Father was throwing firebrands among them. With squeals of rage and astonishment they came tumbling out, filling the air with the smell of singed fur. Their leader, who was well known to us all as the biggest bully in the neighbourhood, turned on us savagely; only to find, however, that we were no longer easy prey as we formed up to meet his charge, axe in one hand, blazing firebrand in the other. Smoke billowed menacingly from our line of battle, and Lord Bruin suddenly halted in his tracks. His henchmen stared as their champion hesitated and snarled instead of going for us. Then another blazing missile, leaving a curved trail of smoke behind it, sprang out of our little phalanx and took him right between the eyes, briefly setting his bushy brows alight. That settled it. Tears of pain and humiliation running down his nose as he pawed his muzzle, Bruin retreated, and the rest of his crowd retreated with him.

"We've won!" we shouted, overjoyed yet incredulous. "We've *won*!"

"Of course we've won," said Father. "And let it be a lesson to you that nature isn't necessarily on the side of the big battalions. Nature is on the side of the species with the technological edge on the other fellow. That's us—for the moment." He fixed us with a warning look. "I said for the moment. Don't let one success go to your heads. We have a long way to go yet—a long way. But now let us take formal possession of this desirable residence."

So we moved in, and an immense improvement on all our previous lodgings we found it. Several times the bears came back, particularly when they thought Father was out hunting, but they always found a bright, welcoming fire burning in front of the cave, and thought better of it. The lions and the other cats came to have a look too, and then, after examining the fire at a distance, tried to pretend they had a better place of their own anyway and departed with the best dignity they could muster to the sound of our derisive laughter.

"One of these days," said Father, "they'll ask to be allowed to stay by the nice warm fire."

"And we'll say 'On your way, you bum!' " said my brother Oswald.

"Maybe," said Father musingly. "Or we might let them—on terms."

"I'd like a pussy-cat all of my own," piped up my youngest brother, William.

"Don't fill the children with silly ideas," said Mother.

We were a small horde at that time, depleted by the severe hunting which we had suffered before Father brought fire down from the mountain. I suppose there were about a dozen of us to begin the new life together. There was my mother, the chief of the women; but we had five aunts as well. Aunt Mildred was a fat, foolish female who could never throw a stone with the least accuracy; she really belonged to Uncle Vanya but he had thrown her over when he found she was no good at climbing trees either. She had a particular reason for liking the fire, because it brought him back to us from time to time and she could thus keep up the pretence that they were mates still. Aunt Angela was a pleasant enough body, mated to another of my father's brothers, Uncle Ian, of whom we heard a lot when we were small children, but never saw, as he was always travelling abroad. Since he could not send us so much as a postcard to tell us he was alive, and he had not been seen for years, Mother and the other aunts believed that he was dead; but Aunt Angela was sure he would come back. "The laddie will be hame soon," she lilted if his name cropped up in conversation. "He's my wee laddie, a terrible wanderer maybe, but I'd be with him myself, as he kens well, but for my poor heart." Aunt Angela suffered from palpitations.

But she had something to look forward to, which was more than Aunt Aggie, Aunt Nellie and Aunt Pam had. Aunt Aggie had lost her mate to a lion. Aunt Nellie had been widowed by a woolly rhinoceros and Aunt Pam by a boa-constrictor. "He would try to eat it," Aunt Pam complained. "Though I told him it could not possibly be good for him. But would he listen? Not he! It was just the same as eating a grass-snake, he said. Well, at any rate, for goodness' sake cut it up, I said. But no, he wouldn't even do that. Just because I said so, of course. He said *it* never cut up things *it* ate, so why should he? Anything it could do, he guessed he could do too. But of course he couldn't. Not even *half* of it! But when the cussed, obstinate fool had to admit that I was right as usual, it was too late. Let that be a lesson to you." She always told this tale to a child that was choking because it was trying to gulp down too much without chewing it. But at other times her acidulous countenance would be wet with tears; her long nose would turn red as a berry and she would rock her angular body to and fro in an agony of remorse. "I could have cut it off myself after a couple of feet," she moaned. "And then he'd be alive now. I didn't because I thought it would teach him a lesson. I let him go on too long, several feet too long. Oh, Monty, Monty, why did you provoke me so?"

She was a tragic figure then, and Aunt Aggie and Aunt Nellie would sit and talk with her and try to comfort her; this ended with all of them wailing together over the mates they had lost. "Ah, the foine,

foine, upstanding boy that I had," Aunt Aggie would wail. "The lion took ye, Patrick, bad cess to the ould Cromwell!"

The women said any nonsense that came into their heads at such times. "A woolly rhinoceros too," sobbed Aunt Nellie. "It had no business in Africa anyway—nasty, hateful, interfering brute. Why couldn't it have stayed on the Riviera where the ice is? Of course it lost its temper, coming here and getting ridiculously overheated!"

I cannot remember all the children in the litter; some of them in any case were eaten by wolves before they grew up. Closest to me was my brother Oswald, who early showed his remarkable genius as a hunter and trapper of animals and of fish too. When quite young he would hang for hours over the stream watching the fish and trying to catch them, as he saw the birds do. In the end he caught a big one and tried to eat it; and almost died the death of Uncle Monty. It was not till long after that we found a really satisfactory way of eating fish.

"But you *ought* to be able to eat it," he said stormily; "I've seen a leopard eat one."

"You've no business to hang about watching leopards at your age!" snapped Mother. "How dare you, you naughty boy! Go and chip flints."

Oswald gloomily obeyed; unlike Wilbur, there was nothing he hated more. Wilbur had a natural flair for flint-knapping, even when quite young. "Very good, my boy," Father would say, as Wilbur struck the bulb of percussion with a precision astonishing in a lad his age. But, wonderful with flint and quartz, he had little to say for himself, and followed Oswald and me in most things. He fagged for us, carrying our hunting sticks, sharpening our flints, humping home anything we killed; he did most of the digging for small game, and he was the one usually made to rob a bees' nest of its honey for us all.

We also put our other half-brother, Alexander, on these fatigues; but though willing enough, he was apt to be unreliable, for he rarely completed any task unless you kept him in sight and shouted at him when he stopped doing it. It was not that he lacked gumption or persistence; he simply became lost in interest in anything he saw, especially animals. He would go off into a trance, and you had to hit him on the head with a stone and wake him up. He could not explain it himself. His observations of animals were extraordinarily accurate, but he seemed to make them without any clear attempt to relate them to hunting techniques as Oswald did; and he was equally happy watching birds, most of which are, of course, completely useless except in so far as they warn you of the presence of big game. Alexander could sometimes help us on hunting expeditions for this reason. The trouble was, he was just as interested in flycatchers as in ostriches or cattle egrets. "There's a lot in that boy, I'm sure," I heard Father remark to Mother one day, after Alexander had told them that a female rhinoceros always walked exactly behind her mate, "but I have no idea what it is." He often referred to Alexander as "our young naturalist."

I had also a much younger brother, William, but it was Oswald, Wilbur, Alexander and I who made up the gang which helped Father on his hunting expeditions.

Of the girls, my sister Elsie was my greatest chum; we had decided to be mates when we grew up. She was tall and graceful as a young gazelle, and she could run and jump and throw as well as any boy. My mother leaned on her most for cave duties, and as we grew older she seemed to come on our hunting expeditions less and less. I never could understand why Mother always found something urgent for her to do at home just when we were starting out. There was a wistfulness in her large brown eyes when she said to me, "I have to stay and look after the fire and the babies, Ernest, but bring something for me, won't you?" I always did. I kept her the eyes of any kill we made, when they fell to me; or an uncracked marrow-bone; or a leaf full of honey or termite-mash. "Thank you, thank you, darling Ernest," she would say as she popped them into her red voluptuous mouth. "I knew you wouldn't forget me," and then she would throw her arms about me and hug me in delight, and I would feel it well worth while to be denied of the pleasure Elsie was having. I could not imagine doing it for anybody else.

We had three other sisters: Ann, Doreen and Alice; it was settled between us boys that when they were full-grown males Oswald should have Ann (who was a strong girl, well able to carry home game), Alexander should have Doreen (who was motherly and very fond of him), and Wilbur should mate with Alice. It was going to be as simple as that.

CHAPTER 4

The fire gave us light after the sun had gone down, and we learned the infinite luxury of relaxing round it of an evening, chewing our food, sucking marrow-bones and telling stories. These, in the early days, came mostly from Father; and the best of them was the story of how he brought down the wild fire to us. I remember it word for word.

"You all remember," Father said, settling himself comfortably with a stick to sharpen, for he was almost never to be seen idle. "You all remember how badly things were going in those days. We were being hunted and hounded to extinction. You lost uncles,

aunts, brothers and sisters in the massacre. The carnivora had turned on us because of a shortage of ungulate game in this region. I am not sure how this
came about. Perhaps it was caused by a series of dry
seasons which reduced their pasture. Perhaps some
new cattle disease had decimated their numbers. Anyway, once the cats begin to eat us in any quantity
they quickly acquire the taste and the habit of it,
and of course they find us easier to run down.

"You may ask why I did not decide to lead you to
safer areas. Of course I gave this possibility much
anxious thought. But where were we to go? North-
wards, farther into the plains—where the carnivora
could accompany us, taking their toll as we went?
Back to the forest—where even now Vanya is finding
it less and less easy to support life? To me it was
unthinkable that we should sacrifice the efforts of
hundreds of thousands of years of evolution and
Stone Age culture and start all over again as tree-
apes. My old father would have turned in his grave,
which is in a crocodile, if I had betrayed all he stood
for like that. We had to stay, but we had to use our
heads. We had to find some way of stopping the lions
from eating us, once and for all. What was that to
be? In the end I found that this was the key question.
Such is the beauty of logical thought; it enables you

systematically to eliminate the alternatives until you are left with the basic question that must be answered."

Father pulled a charred stick out of the fire and thoughtfully inspected its smoking tip.

"I knew, as we all do, that animals fear fire. We fear it ourselves, being animals like the rest. From time to time we have seen it bubbling and boiling down the sides of mountains, setting forests alight; and then every species flies from it in terror. We run almost as fast as the deer, and peril makes lions and ape-men brothers. We have seen whole mountains explode in smoke and flames and then every animal runs in panic to and fro. It does not occur often; but we know what happens when it does. There is no pain like burning; no death like burning to death. Or so it seems. That being so, my problem was to get the effect of a volcano without being actually blown up myself. What I wanted was a small portable volcano. The general idea came to me with a sudden vivid clarity one night when I was manning the barricades. But the general idea—the theoretical solution—is one thing; a workable application is quite another. Ideas in the head don't chase bears out of caves. I was much elated by the elegance of my theory; but I realized that if I didn't do something more than enjoy it I should infallibly be eaten with the rest of my family.

"How did fire work? My second decisive idea, which came to me some time later, was that I should go up a volcano and see. It was the obvious thing to do, once I had thought of it, and I cursed myself for not having thought of it before, I can tell you. Now I had to do it in the middle of an emergency. But clearly my only hope of finding the sort of limited family-size fire I wanted was to go up a volcano and try to chip a bit off somehow. There was nowhere else to look—no time to think of anywhere else to look. I decided to risk everything on one last throw.

"So up the Ruwenzori I went. I guided myself by the flames coming out of the top, and, skirting the glaciers on one side, climbed steadily. The mountain is encircled with a belt of high forest, mostly camphor and euphorbia, and I got through it as fast as I could, partly on the ground, partly through the trees. At first I had the company of animals—warthogs, monkeys, several cats and the like—and flocks of birds; but gradually as the trees thinned out I found myself more and more alone. A noise of underground rumblings, which reminds one of lion, could be heard. At last I was in a sort of wild savannah country of blackened rocks, patches of grass and stunted trees;

it was deathly cold, and there were even patches of snow. The air was becoming rarefied and I caught my breath in painful gasps. I was now quite alone, save for a Tetratornis circling high above the tree-tops I had left far behind, and looking no larger than an eagle at that distance, while a chill wind blew drearily as I reached a desolate region where my shoulders shook with cold yet the rocks were often painfully hot beneath my feet. I began to wonder why I had come there at all; sheer rock and solidified lava now faced me, and far above, under a pall of black smoke, reared the cracked lips of the crater. The sheer presumption of my quest dawned upon me then: to search for an instrument to singe a lion's whiskers in a place where rocks were burned as if they were so much dead wood. My heart almost failed me; I felt a strong urge to turn tail; but I realized that to return empty-handed was as pointless as not to return at all; and the sheer interest of the scene drew me on.

"My persistence was suddenly rewarded. I found that I could not, as I had intended, climb right to the rim of the crater; the rocks still towered a couple of thousand feet or more above me. I had no choice but to work my way in a spiral round the crater, but as I emerged on the far face of the mountain I saw something which rekindled all my hopes. I saw that it would not be necessary for me to climb to the very top, which might indeed have taken me days, even if I could have survived a night in the open in that place. For I saw now that smoke and vapour were issuing far down on that side of the mountain, only a little higher than I now stood. Fire of some sort must therefore be available lower down, and much farther away from the hazards of the crater itself, glowing and bubbling with thousands of degrees Fahrenheit. I therefore made my way obliquely across the mountainside towards the smoke. There, after no little toil, I beheld a most providential thing. The liquid insides of the mountain were being squeezed out and oozing slowly down its rocky flank. It was as though the mountain had been torn open by an enemy, and its red entrails were being pressed out of the gash; or perhaps the mountain had some sort of bilious attack and was throwing up. This, I believe, brought me nearer to the truth of how the world itself was made; but unfortunately, I had no time to make more than the most hasty observations. What immediately interested me was that when the hot vomit touched a tree which stood in its path, that tree immediately burst into flames.

"Here, then, was what I wanted—a connection between the basic fire in the earth and the portable fire I was seeking. As I watched I presently understood the secret of the thing: for when one tree caught fire, any tree that touched it caught fire afterwards. Here was the principle of fire-transmission, demonstrated in nature. If you touch a fire with something it likes to eat, that thing takes fire. This is all very obvious to you now, but remember I was seeing it for the first time."

Father's stick had ceased smoking, and he began absent-mindedly to scrape the blackened tip with a flake of flint.

"The volcano was the father-fire; the trees were sons and daughters, but they too could become parents of fire in turn if touched with another combustible tree. The simple application of the thing suggested itself to me in a flash. All I had to do was to pick up a fallen branch and thrust it against one of the burning trees and carry it off. I tried this immediately; it was hot work, for the wall of lava emitted a tremendous heat and I had to get to within forty yards of it; but it worked! My branch was on fire! I had fire in my hands. I shouted for sheer joy as I carried the branch away from the burning trees, holding it high in the air, and saw that a small volcano was indeed burning and smoking above my head. With that terrible torch in my hand I knew I could frighten any lion out of his wits. I delayed no longer and hurried off home. It was not until I had gone a mile that I discovered that my flaming branch had stopped flaming, and was no more than a hot black stump which burned my hand.

"So back I went to do some more experiments. A small fire, I saw, soon ate up its food; it must be given more unless it is to die. To carry it, I realized, I would have to work a sort of relay. First I set a branch on fire. Then I carried it as far as I could until it had nearly died, or had burned down to my hand; then I tore a branch down from a nearby tree, set that on fire and carried that; and so on to the next. All perfectly simple and logical when you see it done—but not until you see it. This scheme worked admirably, though I found that there were some trees that do not burn as well as others. But by taking care I reached you all right, carrying the six hundred and nineteenth brand in the series, with which I frightened away the lions and lit a fire of our own within the palisade; the same fire that we brought here, and which has never since died. But even if it did it would be perfectly simple to—"

Father stopped suddenly, staring with his mouth

open at the stick in his hand. "Good gracious!" he gasped. "While I have been talking to you, and not even thinking about it, I have made a most important invention: the heavy-duty hunting spear with the fire-hardened point!"

CHAPTER 5

We were always on the look-out for a good, straight piece of wood to make into a spear with our flint-scrapers, and with them we easily knocked down small game, but their weakness had always been the point. Even to kill a small animal you had to get up very close, because at any distance the point had little penetrative power. But it is difficult to get within five yards of a buck, and we lost far more game than we brought down. Our spears simply bounced off the armour of bigger animals, and getting close to most of them was a dangerous business. The best plan was to attack in packs, and then to follow wounded animals until they were too exhausted to fight; but sometimes one merely followed them until a leopard or a lion pounced on them.

The new, fire-hardened spears made all the difference. They were lethal to zebra, for example, at forty yards, and we regularly practised at targets at seventy yards. I could put a spear through the eyehole of a zebra skull at sixty yards, Oswald at seventy, and even eighty if the spear was a good one. We practised, of course, with blunt spears, because to harden the tips for hunting we had to go back to the fire. After a few throws the tips became blunt. This limited the advantage of the new weapon, admittedly, but its general introduction was followed by a big increase in our food supply. We were not cold and hungry nearly so often.

We began to hunt horse and zebra as the usual thing, taking impala, deer, kongoni, wildebeeste, eland, oryx and sheep whenever we got the chance, of course. We stalked them in the long grass, man-high, which covered the plains, running bent but standing upright to mark our prey. Though the herds set sentinels to warn them, this ability to run low and stand up or climb trees to take bearings told in our favour. The giraffe alone could look over the long grass better than we could, and usually spotted us coming; and then their tremendous turn of speed would carry them out of range. We did not get many of them, but had better luck with chalicotheriums, whose necks were somewhat shorter: but they were more dangerous than giraffe if wounded or at bay, for they could gore you horribly with their spreading antlers. The new spears also made it possible to kill buffalo, but they too are dangerous animals, and at first a good many people lost their lives by sticking spears into them, but not deeply enough. Nobody runs faster than a buffalo, even with a spear sticking into his shoulder.

In the forest we had always hunted pig, warthog, monkeys, duikers and suchlike; but now we could attack the giant boar as well. We tried our new spears on crocodiles and hippopotamuses in the rivers. But they afforded us but little additional security in those dangerous places where, in common with all other animals, we had often to risk our lives for a drink of water.

Like the crocs, we ambushed animals coming down to the rivers and water-holes to drink. Observation of the terror of a surrounded animal, blundering into thornbush and sinking into papyrus swamp, gave us the idea of setting traps. Father was particularly interested in these, but we were not, for to us boys fell the task of digging the pits into which the animals were to fall. Digging a pit ten feet deep, and twelve feet square, means moving nearly fifteen hundred cubic feet of soil, which is no fun when you have only a fire-hardened digging-stick, a horse's shoulder-blade and your bare hands to do it with. Father, how-ever, insisted. What he liked about traps, he said, was their automatic quality. "It's hard work, I know," he agreed, "but the idea is right. All we have to do is to think up some more efficient earth-moving equip-ment." But we never did, and it was a relief to us when later he hit on the idea of suspending a spear, point downwards, between two trees by a rope of creepers in such a way that the rope passed from the spear round and between the trees at just exactly the height of a boar's tusks before it was knotted into position on one side. When the boar broke the rope down came the spear between his shoulders. "The germ of feedback," Father said cryptically, and would have rigged the whole forest with the device but for the risk that we should forget where they were located and spring them ourselves. Uncle Vanya had a narrow escape and came to complain.

We hunted far and wide, with a new self-confi-dence born of our spears and the safety of our fire-defended cave. When we killed, we skinned and cut

up the victim, feasting on the blood, brains and entrails where he fell, to the merry chip-chip-chip of
flint knives being resharpened in relays. Then we
quartered the animal and carried the quarters home
on our shoulders: fine trophies compared with rabbits, badgers, squirrels or small antelope that had so
often been our only bag in the old days. With our
spears we easily drove off any hyaenas that wanted
to join us. With spears, too, we could turn to advantage the civil war between the animals. We would
watch for fights between rhinoceroses or elephants at
mating time and finish off the wounded and exhausted vanquished; then the whole horde would settle on the carcass like vultures and eat their way
through it for an entire weekend. The big axes rose
and fell as the mighty vertebrae were hewn apart and
the huge femurs, massive as the trunks of fallen forest
trees, were split for their rich treasure of marrow.
More efficient hunting permitted the women to stay
more often at home instead of following the hunters
to get their share of the kill. "Woman's place is in the
cave," Father began to say.

We boys joined in the hunt, not only because we
were needed, but because Father considered there
was no alternative to the direct method of education.
From the earliest age, of course, we were grounded

in flint-chipping. A boy who was not actually sleeping or following the hunt ought to be at his flints, in Father's view. He also thought that one could not begin too young. Almost as soon as a baby was born, a pebble was put in each of its little hands, and, after swallowing a few, it soon learned to bang them together in imitation of its elders. "Let us never forget," Father would say, "that everything depends, basically, on our ability to squint. Even though we have hands and stereoscopic vision we could not work flint without focusing." The girls had to chip flints too. "A girl should be able to get her own living," Father said. "Even in these days. A girl who can put a really keen edge on a bit of obsidian will never lack for a mate or a square meal."

So the business of flint-chipping was never done, and Father was never tired of talking about the finer points of the art. When we complained of the fragility of the edges we so laboriously made, for example, he was quick to take us up. "Don't forget," he would say, "that the fragility of flint has made possible the ascent of man. For thousands of years apes used tools before they thought of making them, because an accidentally smashed flint so often provides you with a piece which has a cutting edge, which is yours for the picking up. Then somebody dropped one and saw how it happened, and for thousands more years the art of tool-making was simply the art of dropping a flint on a rock and picking up any useful bits. If you think what you are doing is hard work, just try to get your scrapers that way! At last, instead of dropping the flints, men began to strike them, turning the core round and round at random between blows to find the best facet for the next. That is how we all begin. You know that you don't get one decent flake in ten like that. Modern methods have put an end to such waste of time and material. Now we remove a flake from the side of the core—so!—then we use that surface as a striking platform to get new flakes—so! one! two! three! *four*!—what a beauty! Now do you see how uniform the flakes are, and how much lighter the blow you have to give the flint? And you can vary its force; lightly—so!—for a flake, or harder—so!— when the surface demands it. Now then, I want to see all those flakes retouched, please, before lunch-time."

The second great department of education was the study of the animals which we hunted, and those that hunted us. We had to learn where they lived, what they lived on, how they spent their time, what smells they made, and what language they spoke. From our earliest years we could copy the grunt-grunt of the lion, the way the leopard cleared his throat, the boom-boom of the ostrich, the trumpeting of the elephant, the snort of the rhino and the mournful wail of the hyaena. We learned why the zebras and horses, fleet of foot, dared to neigh so much and why the impala and gazelles kept so quiet. Safe in the trees the monkeys could talk to each other, as we, spear in hand, could do on the ground; but the great herds moved silently, ringed with enemies. We learned where to find the turtle's and the crocodile's eggs, and how to rob the birds of their young broods. We knew how to find the scorpion and destroy his tail before eating him.

We also studied economic botany. Some fruits, some fungi, some roots could be eaten; others could not; pioneers all down the Stone Age had given their lives to discover exactly which were which. Instinct had become too atrophied to warn us. We had to learn the vital difference between the cassava root that nourished and the one that killed; we had to learn which were the prohibited fruit, and keep away from the forbidden tree, *Acocanthera abyssinica*, whose very sap was death.

When we began to hunt horse and zebra as a regular thing we began to think of the big cats less as enemies than as rivals and even models in the same

profession. We watched them on the job: leopards
and cheetahs on the higher hills, lions and sabre-
tooths on the plains, pumas and ocelots and caracals
in the jungle and up the trees; and hyaenas everywhere. We could not but be impressed by the hunting
equipment which they brought to the chase—eyes
that could see and whiskers to feel in the dark, retractable claws to grip prey and climb trees, thirty
powerful teeth, good camouflage when stalking, and
considerable speed, with a top acceleration of up to
seventy miles an hour.

Father admired them as much as anyone, but he
warned us not to overdo it. "It is just specialization,"
he said. "Superb single-purpose hunting machines.
They kill game to perfection. And that's their weakness. There is nothing more for them to do. They
won't evolve much further, believe me. You may
think so, with all that strength and cunning, but I
doubt it, I really doubt it. If the game disappeared,
they would starve; they wouldn't tide themselves over
on coconuts! Some of them have overdone it already:
look at sabre-tooth. He can bite through a rhino's
jugular, but who wants to live on rhino? Those teeth
are dreadfully in his way most of the time. Sabre-
tooth had it all his own way when animals were bigger than they are now, and no doubt he polished

off Brontops, Amebelodon, Megatherium and those other early mammals which my Dad used to tell me about when I was a boy; his sabres made him a power in the land when speeds were much less than they are now, but he trips over the wretched things half the time nowadays. Mark my words: he, for one, is on the way out. The others may be all right for a bit, but the day will come when we shall have them begging for scraps from our table."

We laughed at this, but Father shook his head. "You may laugh, but we shall cut the lion down to size yet. I'm not saying that there are no animals that could beat us to it. But they'd probably be anthropoids. I'm always on the alert for that danger. You never know what's brewing. The important thing, however, is to have a firm grasp on sound principles; and I am pretty sure that the principle of specialization puts a stop to evolution sooner or later. Yet animals are fatally driven to it. Take old chalicotherium, for example. He's not a horse, he's not a deer and he's not a giraffe. His neck is too short to be useful as a look-out or to reach the top foliage of trees when the great herds have eaten up the grass. But it's too long for him to make effective use of his antlers. He hasn't got proper hoofs, so he has no real speed. He's neither one thing nor the other, and the real specialists will push him out."

"But neither are we one thing or the other," I said.

Father's low, beetling brows were furrowed in thought. "That is true, my boy, that is true. We have left the trees and have become beasts of prey; yet we lack the teeth and speed of the cats. All the same our strength lies in being unspecialized. It would be retrograde to go down on all fours and grow our canines. Cats and dogs can hunt: but what else can they do? Nothing whatever."

"But Father, who wants to do anything else?" Oswald demanded.

"I admit that you *are* sort of specialized, Oswald," said Father acidly. "Just the same, I wish you could let your primitive mind dwell on higher things occasionally."

"But what else is there to *do*?" Oswald insisted.

"Wait and see," said Father, compressing his lips. "Wait and see."

CHAPTER 6

Yes, you've done it now, Edward," said Uncle Vanya, as he munched a shoulder of horse.

"So you said before," retorted Father, who was working through a prime side of boar. "What's *wrong* with progress, anyway? Tell me that."

"You call it progress," said Uncle Vanya, throwing an impossible bit of gristle into the fire. "I call it disobedience. Yes, Edward, disobedience. No animal was ever intended to steal fire from the tops of mountains. You have transgressed the established laws of nature. I'll have a little of that antelope now, Oswald."

"I see it as a step forward," Father insisted. "An evolutionary step. Perhaps a decisive evolutionary step. Then why disobedient?"

Uncle Vanya pointed a collar-bone at him accusingly. "Because what you have done has taken you outside nature, Edward. It's damnable presumption, can't you see that? And that's putting it mildly. You were a simple child of nature, full of grace, a part of the natural order, accepting its gifts and its penalties, its joys and its terrors: so keen, so self-sufficient, so *innocent*. You were a part of the mighty pattern of flora and fauna, living in perfect symbiotic relationships, but all moving forward with infinite slowness in the majestic caravan of natural change. And now where are you?"

"Well, where am I?" countered Father.

"Cut off," snapped Uncle Vanya.

"Cut off from what?"

"From nature—from your grass-roots—from any real sense of *belonging*—from Eden."

"And from you?" Father said, smiling.

"Certainly from me," said Uncle Vanya. "I disapprove. I've told you that before. I disapprove with my whole being. I continue as a simple, innocent child of nature. I have made my choice. I remain an ape."

"Have some more antelope?"

"I'll try the elephant, thank you. And don't think you have scored any points *there*, Edward! Any animal under sufficient stress of hunger will turn to unusual food; that is the law of survival. Fruit, roots and grubs are my normal diet, but I am allowed in exceptional circumstances to eat game. I say, this elephant is a bit high, isn't it?"

"It is rather. We're not very good at killing elephant yet. We wounded this one and had to follow it for miles and miles. Then it took days to bring home. It weighs heavy, elephant does. But it lasts you."

"Oh, don't apologize. That would be ridiculous, seeing how utterly improper the whole procedure is. I don't mind if it *is* a bit off. Makes it easier to masticate: you haven't got the teeth for meat, you know, Edward. Spent half the time chewing, the whole lot of you. Most unhealthy."

"Yes, that is a problem, I admit," said Father.

"There you are then! You can't say that nature does not make her commandments absolutely explicit. Thou shalt not be a big-game hunter, because thou hast not the teeth for it. What could be clearer? Or this: Thou shalt not steal fire from the mountain because thou hast a nice furry pelt to keep warm in."

"I haven't," protested Father. "Haven't had for years. Besides, that wasn't the point at all. We had to stop the cats eating us. That was natural, wasn't it? Of course, the fire is a very good thing in other ways now we've got it. Just throw another tree on, Oswald, my boy."

"Thou shalt not eat of the tree of the knowledge of good and evil," said Uncle Vanya sulkily, stepping back.

"Besides, I am not at all sure if we are outside nature yet," said Father. "You haven't answered my point yet. Why *shouldn't* the discovery of fire be evolution, just like the giraffe stretching his neck or the horse getting rid of his toes? I could grow a furry pelt if the ice came down here, I suppose; but it would take an awfully long time; and then when the climate got hot again, it would take another age of discomfort to go back to baldness. It ought to be possible to take one's coat on and off when you want to; there's an idea there, you know, though it might be rather difficult to work out in practice." Uncle Vanya snorted. "As it is, we have fire, and can turn the heat on and off when we like. Adaptation, that is. Same thing as evolution, only we get there quicker."

"That's the whole point, you wretched, would-be man!" cried Uncle Vanya. "Don't you see you've no right to speed things up? Pushing events, that's what you are doing, instead of being carried along by them. Pretending to have will, even free will. Hustling nature. And you can't hustle nature; you'll find that out."

"But it's the same thing," said Father indignantly. "We're just going a little faster, that's all."

"It's not the same thing," said Uncle Vanya. "It's completely different! It's insanely fast. It's trying to do in thousands of years what ought to take millions and millions—if it ought to be done at all, which I think highly unlikely. Nobody was meant to live at this killing pace! Don't tell me it's evolution, Edward —besides it's not for *you* to decide whether you are to go on evolving or not. What *you* are doing, out of your own mouth, is something absolutely different. What you are doing, I deeply regret to say, is trying to better yourself. And that is unnatural, disobedient, presumptuous and, I may add, vulgar, middle-class and materialistic. Now then, Edward," said Uncle Vanya nastily. "Out with it. You think you're fathering a totally new species, don't you?"

"Well," said Father uneasily, "I did just have the thought—"

"I knew it!" cried Uncle Vanya triumphantly. "Edward, I can read you like a—like a—well, I know exactly what you're up to. The pride, the sinful pride of the creature! It will not go unpunished, mark my words. You cannot get away with it. No, and I will tell you why. You are no longer innocent, but you *are* ignorant. You have thrown off your allegiance to nature, and now you think you can steer her by the tail. Well, you'll find it isn't as easy as you think, my dear fellow! Better yourself, eh? Instinct not good enough for you, eh? We'll see where that leads—bless me, what is that beastly boy doing?"

Alexander sprang up guiltily from just behind his uncle and made for the trees. But Uncle Vanya's long arm shot out too quickly for him and in a flash yanked him back by his ear.

"Ow!" yelled Alexander, as his ear was twisted mercilessly.

"What were you doing?" roared Uncle Vanya.

"I—I was just—" sobbed Alexander and broke down. There was a burnt stick in his hand and his whole body was streaked with black.

"This is an outrage!" thundered Uncle Vanya.

"Let me see," said Father, hurrying forward; we all crowded round and followed the direction of Uncle Vanya's infuriated gaze. An astonished cry went up.

There, on the surface of the rock, was Uncle Vanya's shadow, faithfully outlined in charcoal pencil. It was unmistakably Uncle Vanya's shadow: nobody could mistake those huge bent shoulders, those hairy half-flexed knees and shaggy buttocks, that prognathous jaw—above all, that simian arm extended in a typical gesture of denunciation. There was the shadow, fixed and immovable in the most astonishing way, amid all the other shadows dancing and flickering in the firelight.

"What is it?" demanded Uncle Vanya in a terrible voice, though there could be but one disastrous answer.

"R-representational art," squeaked Alexander.

"Horrible child," Uncle Vanya yelled. "What have you done to my shadow?"

"You've still got it—or you've grown another very quickly, Vanya," said Father soothingly. "Can't you see?"

"Ah," said Uncle Vanya, his wrath abating somewhat. "Yes, so I have. But I will not have my shadow cut off, even for an instant, by your murderous brats, Edward. I might have been very seriously injured. And you've got no right to that one, either. I want it back—at once, do you hear?"

"Pick it up and give it to him, Alexander," said Father severely, and the miserable Alexander tried.

"I can't," he snivelled. "I can rub it out, though." To our amazement, the shadow disappeared under Alexander's dirty foot. "It was only a. picture," he said.

"Only a picture!" exclaimed Uncle Vanya. "That beats all, that does. You see, Edward? You can't control this thing, which you are pleased to call progress. Thou shalt not make a graven image of thine uncle," he hissed in the tortured and terrified ear of Alexander.

"It was bad manners, Vanya," said Father, "and I will beat him, but I don't think the boy meant any real harm."

"Didn't mean any real harm!" gasped Uncle Vanya. "Edward, you're a simpleton. This is a generation of vipers. I am going."

"Where?" asked Father, innocently.

"Back to the trees!" shouted Uncle Vanya. "Back to nature!"

Father beat Alexander, but not, one could observe, with any real conviction. "Don't draw round people's shadows, my boy," he said. "It's not done. It is easily misunderstood and leads to unpleasantness. At this stage of cultural development we must walk warily in such matters. However, that does not mean that your—ahem—powers of self-expression need to be entirely suppressed. I will think it over."

Later on Alexander and Father spent a lot of time together at a place where the rocks fell sheer to the ground; every now and then one or the other would return to the fire and collect half-burnt sticks. When we tried to see what they were doing, they shooed us away. But at last they returned triumphantly to the cave, some days later, and cried, "Now you can all come and see!" and we flocked to the rock-face. There, magnificent, life-size and bristling, stood a great black mammoth! The aunts screamed and fled in terror; children shot up trees in all directions. Oswald, Wilbur and I alone were armed; at once we discharged our spears. "Behind the tips of the ears! Throw for your lives, lads!" roared Oswald; but the mammoth stood unperturbed as the spears bounced off his hide. Then we saw that Father and Alexander were doubled up with laughter.

"Never mind," said Father. "We have established an important psychological principle."

"But it *is* a mammoth," said Oswald. "I could swear—"

"What?" asked Father.

"I saw it move," mumbled Oswald.

"Exactly," said Father.

"It's a mammoth's shadow," I said. "But where is the mammoth?"

"I bet we wounded him," said Oswald. "We ought to go and track him down."

"I think you had better draw an antelope next time," Father said to Alexander. "Hunting types have dreadfully literal minds."

Nevertheless, soon afterwards Oswald and I went after a mammoth, and we bagged him! He was the dead spit of the shadow. And then a most significant thing happened: the shadow on the rock disappeared. It seemed strange to me that we could eat the mammoth without affecting his shadow, and the morning after we had eaten him I went to throw a spear or two at the shadow. It was a lovely morning, bright and crisp and golden after rain. The shadow was gone. I rushed back and broke the news.

Father was angry; he simply didn't believe me, but he had to admit I was right. He goggled at the bare rock for about an hour and then he said, "There's a perfectly simple natural explanation."

"Of course there is, Father," I said. "The shadow is inside us along with the mammoth."

"Ernest, my boy," said Father. "With a subtle

brain like yours, you may go far. Too far, probably. Go and chip flints until I tell you you can stop. We mustn't let that brain get overheated."

It was deadly, repetitive work for an intellectual. And my release didn't come for a long, long time.

CHAPTER 7

I had not thought Alexander of much serious account until this sudden burgeoning of his talent, but now I felt for him a growing respect. He quickly became adept at trapping the shadows of all sorts of animals on the rocks, and his art drew large and appreciative audiences. I satisfied myself that a significant correlation between shadow-capture, shadow-spearing and subsequent kill could be demonstrated. It was immediately obvious to me that this had implications of great practical value—stupendous possibilities, in fact. Father brooded to what seemed to me an inexplicable extent on the way Alexander's work faded as a result of our hunting.

"Masterpieces," he would say sadly. "Superb primitives. And all doomed. The technique brilliant, the composition robust, but the medium impermanent, the surface unprepared and unprotected; my poor boy, posterity will never give you the credit your work deserves. I doubt if it would last much better in the cave, but why don't you draw inside?"

"Because I can't see a thing in there," said Alexander shortly.

"Oh, for company's light and water," said Father, and went away sighing.

Nobody could have called Father a temperamental type, and most of the time he was cheerful, brisk and busy, finding jobs for everybody, supervising everything. Now he was discussing with the aunts the scraping and dressing of skins; next he was studying the tensile properties of creepers; or puzzling over the uses to which discarded antlers could be put.

"The secret of modern industry lies in the intelligent utilization of by-products," he would remark frowning, and then in a bound he would seize some infant crawling on all fours, smack it savagely, stand it upright, and upbraid my sisters: "When will you realize that at two they should be toddlers? I tell you we must train out this instinctual tendency to revert to quadrupedal locomotion. Unless that is lost all is lost! Our hands, our brains, everything! We started walking upright back in the Miocene, and if you think I am going to tolerate the destruction of millions of years of progress by a parcel of idle wenches, you are mistaken. Keep that child on his hind legs, miss, or I'll take a stick to your behind, see if I don't."

But about this time he seemed to fall into fits of depression and discouragement. This puzzled us, for we had never seemed so prosperous. We lads would return from hunting expeditions laden with game, and Father would only glower at us and say: "Well, well, antelope, baboon, hartebeeste. Very toothsome, no doubt, but what have you done that is *new*?" We would recount the story of the chase and Father would listen attentively with the women; but always at the end he would say: "Yes, yes, but it's the same old thing, you know. What have you done that's *new*?"

"But, Father, what can we do that's new in hunting?" Oswald protested. "We do it the way you taught us. Do you want us to go after lion?"

"No, no, I didn't mean that; you know I didn't,"

Father replied pettishly. "You can't go after lion until you have—well, that's just the point. Are you satisfied with your equipment?"

"Of course, Father," said Oswald.

"And you, Ernest—what progress have you made?" Father would exclaim impatiently, turning on me. "You're practically grown up, you know!"

"Well, Father," I said. "I was thinking about making magic with shadows—"

"Pshaw!" snarled Father. "And these are my grown sons! William—well, I suppose you're too young for exams."

"I've got this," piped up William unexpectedly.

"What's that?" demanded Father sharply, and William held up a small, struggling object.

"It's a dog-cub," said William. "A puppy. I call him Rags."

"Be careful he doesn't give you indigestion," said Mother. "They get dreadfully tough in no time at all with all that running. You'd better eat him quick, but chew him well, dear."

"But I don't want to eat him," cried William tearfully.

"Throw him over here, then," said Oswald.

"No!" screamed William. "I don't want to. I don't

want *anyone* to eat him. He's mine! You're none of you to eat him, do you hear? Poor little Rags."

"He's gone clean off his chump," gasped Oswald.

"The whelp will bite him, Father," I said. "Shall I take it from him?"

"No, don't you dare, Ernest," William cried. "I'll tell him to bite *you*."

"He was always an hysterical little boy," said Aunt Nellie soothingly. "He used to get these fits much more often when he was younger. Now just leave him to me, William dear, doggies do bite. And they have such dirty habits, you know. Let me cut him up for you and you can have him all to yourself for supper."

"I hate you! I hate you!" yelled William, and the dog began to yap furiously.

"Now just a minute, just a minute," said Father as Oswald rose threateningly. "There's more in this than meets the eye. Sit down, Oswald. Calm yourself, William. So you won't eat the dog. Very well, you don't have to. But what you are going to do with him?"

"I—" William gulped. "I was going to bring him up, Father. His mother got killed and so did all his brothers and sisters. He's quite alone in the world, and too young to join the pack. He's quite friendly—

most of the time. I thought he could grow up with me, and we could be friends always."

"But what on earth is the point of that?" demanded Oswald impatiently. "Even if he would, he'd only grow too tough to eat. Be your age!"

"That will do, Oswald," said Father. "Kindly leave this to me. Now, William, I have not said you were naughty. But you must see sense. What good will it be, my boy, having a great yellow snarling dog for a friend? He'd grab your meat, sure as eggs are eggs."

"I wouldn't mind," said William obstinately. "Not while he was young. When he grew up he could come hunting with me, and we could share the kill. He'd be very helpful on a hunt, 'cos he can run fast."

"Well," shouted Oswald with a great laugh. "Of all the idiotic ideas—"

"Quiet, Oswald," snapped Father. "Quiet, all of you! This is not as silly as you suppose. Just let me think—William, I am not sure but I believe you *have* hit on something new after all. Dog, the faithful friend of man. Men and dogs, hunting. Mm, yes, by dingo, it *could* make sense. It could make a lot of sense! Hounds, terriers, spaniels, pointers, retrievers —the possibilities are stupendous! William, what exactly is the state of the relationship between you and that mongrel?"

"Well," said William defensively, "I'm teaching him to beg. He nearly can."

"Let me see," said Father.

We all gathered round William. He held the dog down on the ground by the scruff of its neck with one hand, and with the other held the drumstick of an ostrich three feet above it.

"He has to sit on his hind legs," explained William, "and hold up his front paws, and wait till I give him the drumstick. Later, I shall teach him 'trust' and 'paid for'—that means he mustn't touch a bit of meat until I say 'paid for' after I have said 'trust.' Then I shall teach him 'please' and 'thank you,' and after that I shall teach him 'to heel' and after that—"

"Yes, yes," said Father. "I see you have thought the whole system out most thoroughly, William. But now let's see him sit up and beg."

"All right," said William doubtfully. "Now, Rags, beg! Beg, Rags, good doggie!" All this time the puppy had been squirming, snarling and snapping in William's grasp. Now William let go, and things happened in a flash. Rags leapt up and bit William savagely on the hand. William, with a squeal of "Naughty, Rags!" dropped the drumstick. Rags pounced on the drumstick, and shot between Oswald's legs. Oswald smote at Rags, missed him, and with an explosion of profanity caught his knuckles hard on the rocky floor of the kitchen-midden. I, who had vaguely foreseen something going wrong, had provided myself with a stick and swiped at Rags, but caught Alexander hard behind the knees. Alexander collapsed backwards, and in falling gave Aunt Pam a sharp blow in the belly with his elbow. Aunt Pam sat down hard in the embers, screamed, seized Aunt Mildred by the hair to help herself up. Aunt Mildred screamed too, and the aunts then began to keen together, while Mother applied plaintain leaves to Aunt Pam's posterior. My sister Elsie, who had alone got away after the dog, returned panting.

"He got away," she said.

Nor did we ever see Rags again, though William went after him the moment he had made hurried apologies all round.

"Well, there you are," said Father later. "I am afraid it was too big a job for you, William. What a pity."

"I'm sure I started the right way," William said, snuffling and licking his hand. "You must catch them young and treat them with kindness."

"I dare say," said Father dryly. "But the trouble is, what do you do then if they continue to behave like wild beasts? That's the problem. If that wound on your hand goes septic, you'll die and be a martyr to progress," he added kindly. "So don't be too discouraged, my boy. It's quite something to be ahead of your time at your age. You and Alexander have done very well lately. I only hope this early promise will not be dissipated when you are older by excessive addiction to the excitement of the chase." He glared at Oswald and me. "Let this be a lesson to you older boys. We have a lot of thinking to do, a lot to learn and a long, long way to go. We must not, we dare not, relax. Yet, I ask you, where exactly *do* we go from here?"

"You have a lot of chewing to do," Mother said. "If you don't finish this elephant it will become totally uneatable."

"You have got a point there, my dear," Father admitted, helping himself to a rib. "I'm not sure that you have not touched the heart of the matter. It is something which has been worrying me for some time. Very roughly, I calculate that we spend a third of our time sleeping, a third of our time catching meat, and the whole of the remaining third eating it. Even so, we have none too much time for eating. My heartburn has been extremely troublesome lately. But that only lends emphasis to my point. When we are so tied down by the mere routine of getting a living, what time have we to think? It is no use telling me that chewing is conducive to rumination; it isn't—not the chewing we have to do, anyhow. To broaden our minds and take a longer, more considered view of our objectives we need some peace from the grinding of our mandibles. Without a meed of leisure and quiet there can be no creative work, no culture, no civilization."

"What is culture, Father?" asked Oswald, his mouth full of elephant.

"You may well ask," Father replied, heavily. "There are none so blind as those that will not see."

"But how far *have* we to go, Father?" I asked. "I thought we were very comfortable here."

"Nonsense," snorted Father. "Comfortable? You'll be saying that we are properly adjusted to our environment next. That's what they all say when they get tired of evolving. That's the last thing your specialist says before an even more specialized specialist comes along and gobbles him up. How many times must I tell you these things, Ernest? There are moments when I get the feeling that there is a clear and unobstructed passage between your ears. And you call yourself the crown and consummation of a million years of evolutionary toil by your betters. Pshaw!"

"Well," I said, feeling my ears getting rather red, "how far have we to go, anyway?"

Father put down his elephant, and placed the tips of his fingers together.

"That," he said, "depends on where we are now."

"Where are we?" I asked.

"I am not sure," said Father, his voice suddenly low and sad and grave. "I am not sure. I *think* about the middle of the Pleistocene. I doubt if we have reached the Upper Pleistocene yet. I wish I could think so, Ernest, but looking at you, listening to you, I cannot think it. Now if Alexander or William could pull off something—but I fear their ideas outrun their experience by a long chalk. As a matter of fact," his voice sank almost to a whisper. "As a matter of fact, there have been moments lately when I have had doubts if we've got beyond the Early Pleistocene yet."

"You've been working too hard, dear," said Mother, patting his hand. "I wish you could take a little holiday." My father's face was a mask of tragedy, or tortured self-distrust, at that moment. He fell completely silent, and there was nothing to be heard but the crackle of the fire and the crackle of the lice (*Pediculae antiquae*) as the women preened each other's long, lank hair. To relieve the embarrassment in which we found ourselves, I spoke again.

"How, Father," I asked, "can we find out where we are?"

Father roused himself. "By indirect means only, my son. There are signs for those who know how to read them. Let me give you an example. If we ever run into an hipparion, the three-toed horse, we shall know that we are barely out of the Pliocene, merely at the beginning of our long, long upward struggle. Then indeed you will have to put your backs into it! Nobodies, that's what you'll be, relatively speaking, mere nobodies."

"I've never seen an hipparion," said Oswald.

"I trust you never will," said Father. "All the same, they tend to linger on, these obsolete models, you know. I dare say they lasted into the Lower Pleistocene, after all. Look at old chalicotherium! Plenty of them about, even now."

But though Father seemed to be comforted by this reflection, I did not dare to discuss the question with him further. He was morose and out of sorts for weeks afterwards. I could not imagine what he was so worried about. I could not believe that the exact point which we had reached in geological time was so important. What was the need to hustle? Everything seemed to be going very well. The sun fed and the rain refreshed the busy, workaday world. The earth throbbed and trembled under our feet; the volcanoes rumbled away industriously, pouring out lava and coils of thick, black smoke. Sulphurous smells often lay heavy on the air, and when the clouds rolled in upon Africa as the ice-caps drove south, we had bouts of choking smog. The geysers in the mudflats gurgled and bubbled; jets of steam hissed from the safety-valves down on the thin valley floors. The forests marched up the mountains, the mountains boiled over and hurled the greenery back again. Every plant was hard at it competing for the custom of the birds and the bees; the fashions in flowers and fruit followed each other in bewildering variety. Every species was hard at it, trying to outbreed and outwit every other species and make good its claim to be the fittest to survive. The enlightened self-interest of each individual harmonized to produce the greatest food for the greatest number. Ah, sweet Monday morning of the world! Ah, Africa, most progressive of continents, cradle of subhumanity! Sufficient unto the day the labour and the magic thereof, thought I; we were artificers of stone, tamers of fire—and we could snap our fingers at anyone, practically. Things looked pretty good to me.

But Father would not have been Father if he hadn't wanted something better. He was not at all happy

about the results of his experiments to extend the use
of fire. For some time he had been saying that we
ought not just to import fire ready-made from volcanoes, but should manufacture it ourselves.

"It is ridiculous," he said, when our cave fire had
gone out for the tenth or ten-thousandth time (I forget which). "It is ridiculous that every time your bird-
brained aunts let the furnace out I should have to
climb a 15,000-foot mountain. At my age too. It's a
bit much. But as there is no hope of improvement in
your aunts, or your revered mothers either, something else must be done."

"But perhaps fire just can't be made," I objected.
"Spontaneous combustion may be a fallacy. Or it
may be magic—"

"Pshaw!" said Father. "Look at that, you le-
muroid! Do you never ask yourself what *that* is?"

He pointed to the flints which Wilbur was knap-
ping. Every now and then a spark or two flew from
the impact of the stones. Of course we had all seen
this happen; but until then I had never connected it
with that hot and furious thing, the fire. It was like
comparing a reed-rat and a mammoth. I had reached
the conclusion (which I did not try out on Father)
that it was the life in the stone, the stone's soul. If it
was fire—this presented all sorts of difficulties, such

as that stones could burn. They can, growled Father. "Seen 'em do it." He brushed my ideas aside as always. But he became extremely excited when Wilbur told him that he had noticed that some sorts of stone produced more sparks than others. Father insisted that if you could carry fire from sparking wood you could carry it from sparking stones; the principle was exactly the same. I saw the force of this argument; but I also saw how woefully it broke down in practice. For Father could not catch the occasional tiny sparks that flew from Wilbur's flints; and when he threw the flints into the fire in fury, they merely put the fire out.

He tried this, he said, because if you hit the flint often enough and hard enough, it gets warm and angry at its treatment. He found out that this was as true of inanimate objects generally as of his own sons; if he banged one stick on another hard enough, they both got hot with anger and exertion. He thought that he was on the very brink of success then, and expected the sticks to burst into flames at any moment. But they would not. He was only solaced by the discovery that if you blew on dead embers they would sometimes re-ignite. He got this idea from the wind. But beyond this point he was baffled. The embers had always to have come from a fire born of a volcano at some remove. Month after month passed, and still he laboured. But he could not find out how to start a fire with either stones or sticks. It seemed to prey on his mind. Panting, he would desist from his exertions and turn on me savagely.

"Ernest! Why don't you *do* something? Am I never to have any help from you? Here, take this stick and beat the other till it's hot—hot, I said!"

So I did as he ordered me, but I knew it was futile. I was no volcano, and soon grew tired. Then Father would prod me with some antlers, which hurt very much in several places, and I would set to again. But we weren't getting anywhere. Father knew it as well as I did.

Soon after that, Uncle Ian returned.

CHAPTER 8

He was a stocky little man, with bandy legs, red hair and a rather thin, red beard, bright blue eyes, and scars all over his body, each and every one of which led to an exciting story when you said, "How did you get that one, Uncle Ian?"

Aunt Angela saw and scented him coming a long way off, rushed from the cave like a spear in flight, crying, "My own wee laddie!" and led him triumphantly into our midst.

"Well, Ian," said Father, putting his arm round Uncle Ian's broad shoulder and giving him a brief hug. "Well, Ian, it's good to see you again."

"Welcome home, Ian," said Mother, and we all chorused, "Welcome, welcome, welcome, Uncle Ian."

Uncle Ian ceremoniously went round the whole family circle repeating everybody's name and making sure he knew who was who. "Ah, Pam, I've not forgotten poor Monty; Aggie, not a day older, my dear, not a day; Nellie, you've mellowed, I do believe you've mellowed; and who is this—Oswald? Great Deinotheriums! Have I been away as long as that? Why, ye're a man, Oswald! Ech? Ernest? Nay, I can't call ye to mind, lad; but I have the smell of you, and I won't forget it again—aye, and a queer, cross-grained smell it is too, like an elephant plotting mischief. Alexander? William? You're all a new lot. Well, well, you've got a fine place here, I must say."

Then Father took Uncle Ian round the domain and showed him all our improvements; and above all, of course, the fire.

"They've got it in China too," said Uncle Ian.

"What!" exclaimed Father. "I don't believe it!"

"Aye, they have," Uncle Ian repeated. "They're always first with everything."

"Can they *make* it?" asked Father anxiously.

"I shouldna wonder," said Uncle Ian, but Father had noticed his hesitation.

"I bet they haven't," he snapped. "We're definitely ahead technologically."

"Why, can you?" asked Uncle Ian.

"Not exactly," said Father. "But when the present series of experiments is concluded, I confidently expect to be able to announce—"

"Aye," said Uncle Ian, and sucked a hollow tooth. "How's Vanya these days?"

"Up a tree," said Father crossly.

We plied our long-lost uncle with the choicest viands we had: prime ribs of mammoth; collops of chalicotherium; haunches of horse and zebra; shoulders of lamb; and boar's head. For garnishing we added baboons' brains, crocodiles' eggs, and turtles' blood, of which Aunt Angela remembered he had always been very fond.

"A first-rate dinner," Uncle Ian said finally, as the last marrow-bone dropped from his fingers. "I've not done so well since I was at Choukoutien."

"China, I suppose?" growled Father. Uncle Ian nodded.

Then, of course, he had to tell us the story of his travels. We heaped up a mountain of branches to feed the blaze; we supplied ourselves with bones to gnaw, spears to point or, in the case of the women, skins to scrape and sinews to collect; and squatted round him. It was an epic tale that required days and weeks for the telling; I can but give the bones of it. Uncle Ian was the greatest traveller I have ever known; wanderlust and walkabout were in his blood; he had visited nearly every country under the sun, and shrewdly observed everything that was to be seen. It was no wonder that he had been away so long.

"It is no use to go south in Africa," he said. "You come to a pretty country, but a dead end, a sack, with nothing beyond but the salt sea. It's a backward place, and the people are backward too. You see what looks like a promising ape-man there; standing pretty well as upright as we do, swaggering along with broad shoulders and head held high. But when he turns round, och, what a disappointment. He's got no brain-case to speak of, and the face of a gorilla under it. Hasn't got much more than the vocabulary of a gorilla either, twenty or thirty words, I suppose. His flints are pathetic; just pathetic."

"Doesn't sound as if *he'd* come to much," said Father, rubbing his hands with satisfaction.

"I have my doubts," agreed Uncle Ian, and went on: "No, in Africa you've got to go north. There's easy hunting, easy feeding, plenty of water all the way. There's thickish forest at first, and it's infernally hot; the folk there, by the way, are going in for black skins—"

"What an extraordinary notion!" exclaimed Father. "Why?"

"They think it keeps the sun off better and makes it harder to see them under the trees," said Uncle Ian.

"They're making a very great mistake," said Father. "No good will come of that. The only sensible colour for human skin is dark brown or serviceable khaki—the colour of the veldt, the colour of lions. I regard that as settled from an evolutionary point of view. Next thing you will be telling me you met with some hominid species going in for *white* skins!"

When the gale of laughter produced by this sally had died down, Uncle Ian continued his narrative.

"Bide a wee, bide a wee," he said. "There's climates and climates. Beyond the tropical forests, when you get to the Sahara, why it's an earthly paradise! Lovely green, rolling country as far as the eye can see, intersected by great rivers and countless streams of pure, running water, teeming with fish. Glorious mountains, clothed in oaks and beech and ash. And what grazing! Lush grass to the horizon, sparkling with flowers of every hue. Horse, zebra, eland, antelope, sheep, cattle—herds without number. Every prospect pleases."

"Hordes?" inquired Father.

"Aye, the species is well established, Edward. Hunting territories well marked out, though not without some bickering, at times. But there's enough for all and more. Go north, young man," he added, turning to Oswald, whose eyes where shining. "There's a new life waiting for ye in the wide-open spaces of the Sahara. I nearly stayed there myself. But I didna; I went on.

"After a time you come to the biggest lake of all, a lake far bigger than any in Africa, running east and west, that seems to bar the way. But I went west-wards along the shore of it, where ape-men live very comfortably on shellfish alone, until I came to an isthmus between the lake and the salt ocean in which the sun sets. The traffic is very heavy there, with mammoths, wolves and bears going north, and streams of hippos and giraffes and lions and I don't know what coming south. It's getting far too cold for them in Europe. I found it distinctly chilly myself when I crossed the Pyrenees, and I saw snow heavier there than on the Mountains of the Moon. And when I looked north I could see the ice, by the trillion ton, bearing down."

"Yes, I know it's an ice-age," said Father glumly.

"The trouble is—which? Gunz? Mindel? Riss or Wurm? It makes all the difference, you know."

"I dinna ken," said Uncle Ian. "I know just how cold it was, that's all! I went down into the valleys of the Dordogne and found reindeer running everywhere."

"What are reindeer?" asked Oswald.

"Oh, a deer built to stand ultra-low temperatures," said Uncle Ian. "As I was saying, the reindeer were running about everywhere, and the Neanderthaloids were running after them."

"Another species of hominid?" asked Father excitedly.

"I'm not so sure about the hominid," retorted Uncle Ian. "They're a remarkable species, anyway. Different from us, certainly. Hairy they are, hairy all over like giant goats; and they need to be to turn the frosty wind! They are not a tall lot; but not diminutive either; I had an inch or two on them, which made it easier for us to get on together. Broad, reverberating chests, they have, and they walk more like apes than we do, with bent knees and on the outer sides of their feet like babies. They have hardly any necks: their heads are set between their shoulders, and their foreheads are villainously low. But that does not mean that there is no grey matter behind them. Oh dear me, no! You can see the brain positively bulging out over their ears. I make them an intelligent crowd. They do a bonny flint, a very bonny flint indeed! They have some funny ideas, though; that's what comes of those long nights dreaming and story-telling in the caves."

"What sort of funny ideas?" Father asked.

Uncle Ian shook his head. "Too metaphysical for me, I'm afraid. I'm the practical type. But they bury their dead."

"I call that improvident," said Father.

"They think of it the other way round," said Uncle Ian.

"And I don't like the idea of the hair," Father added. "Too specialized."

"It's their teeth that worry them most," said Uncle Ian. "Bad teeth they have; martyrs to toothache, most of them. Arthritis, too. They'd walk straighter, I shouldna wonder, but for that. It's a terrible damp climate."

"I wonder just when they left the parent anthropoid stem," mused Father. "Sometime in the Pliocene, at latest, I fancy. Are unions with them fertile, do you know?"

"I won't be certain till I get back," said Uncle Ian

cautiously. "But I have some reason to think so. I got on with the girls well, for all that they called me 'baby-face.' "

"They would," Father said, placing the tips of his fingers together in a typical gesture and clearing his throat. "Our development is paedomorphic, you see, and—"

"Aye. Well, from France I had to bear due eastwards again," continued Uncle Ian, "skirting the steppe and the tundra by keeping close to the great lake. I found *Homo neanderthalensis* pretty well dug in throughout the Balkans. It was hard work, going from cave to cave; but in the end I came to Palestine. There I found the Neanderthaloids fighting with immigrants coming from Africa."

"Why? Shortage of game?" asked Father.

"No, no, it's a bountiful country, flowing with milk and honey," said Uncle Ian. "But there's something in the air there that makes primates as cantankerous as gorillas that have eaten sour apples. So fighting they were, but mating too."

"It's much the same thing," said Father. "H'm, I wonder what will come of it? Hairy apes and hairless apes miscegenating in Palestine in the Pleistocene?"

"Bearded prophets living on locusts and honey in the Holocene," I suggested.

"Don't try to be smart, Ernest," growled Father. "You're not cut out for it. Go on, Ian. Where did you go next?"

"India, *via* Arabia," Uncle Ian replied. "Arabia is a luxuriantly green country, like the Sahara; but oh! how it *rained*! In India, I met a new carnivore, the tiger, burning bright in the forests of the night. It's a tremendously pepped-up version of Smilodon. Give me old sabre-tooth every time! I spent most of the nights in the Indian forests right up at the top of the trees, and I'm not ashamed of it either! A bit farther on I ran into another variety of the subhuman family."

"Another?" gasped Father.

"Another," said Uncle Ian, nodding. "But nothing for you to worry about, Edward. Leftovers from the Miocene, I should think. Hopelessly out of date. About half our size, and the brain of a monkey, or not much more. Eyes under big bony ridges, and nothing to call a brain-case behind them. I'd have called them monkeys, but for the fact that they walked upright and had fully triangular jaws so that they could talk quite well—in pidgin, admittedly, "Dat ape im belong big big spear" kind of stuff. I dare say they would have made good enough bearers, if I'd had time to train them, or anything for them to carry. But after slaughtering a few I had to get on.

"Well, then, Edward, I reached China at last, and there I found the prototypes of the Chinese, living in caves round Choukoutien. I thought they were gorillas at first, but I was wrong. They stood up much more, and they made quite a serviceable flint. Quite serviceable enough to cut each other up with, anyway."

Father nodded. "Waste not, want not," he said, glaring round the family circle.

"They had got this wild fire from somewhere too," said Uncle Ian, "and were pretty proud of it. But frankly I think they were static. That's always the tendency among Orientals. They told me there was a bigger size, in the same design, farther north in the snows of Tartary. About fifteen feet high, and hairy as a bear. I decided not to try to make acquaintance with anything so abominable. I had quite enough of Sinanthropus as it was. Besides, I wanted to see how things were shaping in America."

"Ah, yes, America!" said Father enthusiastically. "How did you find it there?"

"I didn't," said Uncle Ian sadly. "There's an icy curtain between them and the rest of the world. You can't get through. Not even *Homo neanderthalensis*. The place is overrun with glyptodons—what isn't under ice, of course."

"That's bad news, Ian," said Father. "Very bad news. It means we're not nearly as far on as I'd hoped. No Americans *yet*? I can hardly believe it."

"Well, that was some time ago," said Uncle Ian. "It may be possible to get through by now. In fact, I'm going back to try to find the north-east passage."

"No, no, no," screamed Aunt Angela, "and you so sore worn with your wanderings! Bide and rest, and dinna leave me again!"

Uncle Ian comforted her, but I could see his eyes were far away. I knew he would not stay with us long. But, alas, the end came sooner than we expected.

He showed extraordinary interest in William's experiments in the domestication of animals, and when Father said, "He's before his time, you know, Ian; we just have not got that far," Uncle Ian said, "I can think of an animal that would be verra, verra useful to me, if it were biddable."

Then, one morning, there was an uproar. An extraordinary animal charged into our little settlement —a man-horse, neighing, whinnying, curveting, bucking and belching oaths and shouts of "Whoa, my lass!" and "Steady, you brute!" It reared furiously as it reached the fire, scattering members of the family in all directions. Then, for a moment we saw what it was: no centaur, but Uncle Ian on horseback. But at that moment Uncle Ian left the horse, went sailing through the air, and circled to earth with a deadly thud. We rushed to him, but he was past hope; his neck was broken.

As the horse dashed away, however, Oswald caught it with his spear right between the shoulders and it, too, sank lifeless to the earth.

And now we found we had a double tragedy on our hands. Uncle Ian, the mighty traveller, was dead, with Aunt Angela swooning over his body; and the horse he had tried to ride—to get to America the quicker—proved not to be a horse at all: it was an hipparion.

CHAPTER 9

Soon after we had recovered from Uncle Ian's funeral, Father called Oswald, Alexander, Wilbur and me together, and told us we were to accompany him on an expedition. We assumed that he meant hunting, but something in his manner told me that he had unusual business in mind. For days he had squatted apart by himself, growling angrily when anyone came near him, and doing nothing, which was quite unlike him. The discovery that hipparions were not yet extinct had been a very heavy blow, and I noticed that his hair was now streaked with grey.

But on that morning all his customary cheerfulness had returned, and he moved about briskly as he helped us to make preparations, sharpening spears in the fire, selecting stone knives for the journey, and leaving Mother with a mass of instructions.

Then he led us out eastwards through the jungle. This soon showed that we were not going to be given a further course in the handling of volcanoes, since the Mountains of the Moon were behind us and he by-passed Mount Kenya and Ngorongoro's belching flames. I hardly imagined that he meant to go as far as Kilimanjaro, which was no fierier than they. Nor did he seem in any hurry to give chase, though time and again Oswald and I scented game. He called us sharply to heel, and on and on we went. It was not until nightfall that he allowed us to knock down an okapi for supper. We had no fire, and had to keep watch by turns.

The next day was the same, and the next; it was clear that we were bent on some very special quest, but Father was in no mood to satisfy our growing curiosity. Though he was in a good mood so long as we kept together, the dead-straight line in which we were travelling and the determined look in his eye gave me an unpleasant sense of foreboding. On the fifth day, however, we relaxed. We ceased to march with the compulsive discipline of a file of ants; Father began to sniff the wind and to cast this way and that to catch a scent. So it was a hunt after all! We all joined in, but though Oswald repeatedly found scent, Father would have none of them. "Buffalo, Father?" Oswald would call out, but Father shook his head. "Well, then, zebra? horse? elephant? giraffe?" But Father refused them all, and with his own nose up sought for something none of us had thought of. At last, when Oswald called out despairingly, "Mastodon?" Father said: "Don't be silly. I think I've got it now: yes, that's them."

We all put our noses up in his direction, and certainly there was something, faint and far away to the eastwards, coming and going exasperatingly as the wind veered. It was a familiar scent, too, but before we could identify it, Father said:

"Come on, boys. There's thirsty work ahead; and I can smell water just beyond those trees. We'll have a drink and then I'll tell you all about it."

We lost the scent in the trees as, burning with curiosity, we followed Father to the water.

We came out by a lake, pink with flamingos and water lilies, and soon found a place to drink. There

was plenty of spoor, so we spent some time hurl-
ing rocks at the crocodiles we could see and any
doubtful-looking tree-trunks nearby. Then Father
went in to his knees, bent and drank, soused his dusty
torso and face, and came splashing back.

"O.K., boys. I'll keep watch while you have yours.
Give me the spears."

Within a few moments we also returned to dry
land, much refreshed; but we were astonished to find
that Father had left us totally unguarded, and was
now standing with his back to a cotton tree in a
clearing thirty yards away. Our spears were neatly
stacked between two of its mighty buttresses within
easy reach of his hand, and he faced us with his
own spears, one in each hand, raised and pointed
towards us.

"Halt!" he cried out. "That's near enough! We can
hear each other."

I realized that we faced a crisis.

We halted.

"Now, boys," Father said. "I owe you an explanation. But don't try any monkey-tricks—by which I
mean throwing stones. I have the range of you, and
plenty of ammunition, and you wouldn't stand a
chance.

"Well, now, it's all very simple, and there's no real need to get excited. I have been giving this thought for quite some time, and I have talked it over with your mothers. You four lads have passed puberty. To all intents and purposes you are grown up. You, Oswald, are at least fifteen; Ernest perhaps a year younger, Alexander and Wilbur about the same. You are trained hunters; you know woodcraft, savannah-craft, mountaincraft and all the rest of it. You have been well grounded in flint tool-making, though only Wilbur is really good. You are capable of making your own livings; in addition—a most exceptional advantage in boys your age—you know how to fetch wild fire and how to keep it burning. It is time you found mates and started families of your own for the sake of the species; and that is why I have brought you here. Not twenty miles to the south there is an-other horde—"

"That's what it was!" ejaculated Oswald. "A kitchen-midden! Ape-men! I should have known."

"There is another horde," Father repeated. "And there you will find the mates you want."

"But, Father," I protested. "We don't want strange ape-women for mates. We've got our own girls at home. I'm having Elise, and—"

"No, you're not," Father interrupted. "You're having one of those girls over there."

"But it's absurd, Father," I exclaimed. "We've got it all fixed."

"People *always* mate with their sisters," Oswald said. "It's the done thing."

"Not any more," said Father. "Exogamy begins right here."

"But it's unnatural, Father," I said. "Animals don't make distinctions of that sort, you know. Once in a while one might go outside one's own horde, I suppose, but it can't be called a regular rule."

"It's absurdly inconvenient," added Oswald. "Our girls are there, and these other girls—"

"Are nearer, actually," Father said. "That's why I brought you here."

"I can't see why we should be put to all this trouble," I said. "I mean, what's wrong with the girls at home?"

"Nothing is wrong with them," Father said. "But there would be if you inbred with them. We must mix up the genes a bit. But that is not the main reason. The main reason is that they're too easy; too accessible, too little trouble. They provide too uninhibited an outlet for the undisciplined libido. No; if we want any cultural development, we must put the emotions of the individual under stress. In short, a young man must go out and find his mate, court her, capture her, fight for her. Natural selection."

"But we can easily fight for the girls at home," said Oswald. "In fact, we are sure to. It's the usual thing. Like the animals. The strongest male wins. There's natural selection for you," he added shrewdly, but Father would not have it.

"Not the right sort of natural selection. Not any more. It is getting too dangerous to have fights in the family over women with all these deadly new weapons like fire-tipped spears lying around. It may have been all right when the males just banged each other over the head with old-fashioned clubs."

"It was all right for *you*," I said bitterly.

"Times have changed," said Father. "Or rather, they haven't, and that's the trouble. We are further behind than I thought. It won't do to stick around as contemporaries of the hipparion! *It won't do*. We're stagnating as a species, and that is fatal. We have fire, but we can't make it; we can kill meat but we spend half our time chewing it; we have spears and the extreme range is seventy yards—"

"Ninety-four yards," said Oswald.

"Freak," snapped Father. "I'm talking practicalities. Alexander, you can draw, but you can't fix a line you have drawn. Wilbur, you've been putting some good edges on hand-axes, but—I hate to say it—the stuff we're turning out is very little better than eoliths. Ernest, you think you can think, but you can't, because the range of things we can do is so narrow. That means we don't extend our very small vocabulary and our limited grammar; which in turn means a restricted power of abstraction. Language precedes and breeds thought, you know; and it is really little more than a courtesy to call a language the few hundred substantives we possess, the score of all-purpose verbs, the poverty of prepositions and postpositions, the continued reliance upon emphasis, gesture and onomatopoeia to eke out shortages of cases and tenses. No, no, my dear sons; culturally we are little higher than *Pithecanthropus erectus*; and he, believe me, is no go. You heard what your lamented Uncle Ian had to say about *him*. He's for the dump, along with the rest of nature's failures."

"I always kill them," said Oswald.

"Quite right," said Father. "But we don't want to go the same way that he did. That's why we've got to make an effort. I want you to look at this in a reasonable way, as responsible adults," he added, with a note of appeal in his voice. "It *is* inconvenient. I don't

deny it. It *is* new. It will take some getting used to—
if you ever do. But you can't build up a head of water
without creating barriers, inhibitions, frustrations,
complexes. It's an idea I got from watching beavers.
They stop rivers; and look at the force with which
the water pours through the narrow gap that is left.
Look at the Murchison Falls, for the matter of that;
or, better still, go and look at the Victoria Falls. That
will give you an idea of what I mean—obstruction to
develop irresistible force. Only, we aren't rivers; this
is something which has to be done in our heads."

"I have a cataract going in my head now," said
Wilbur, sitting down and sinking his muzzle between
his hands.

"It is hard to understand at first," said Father.
"But if we are to solve problems—if we are to have
problem-seeing and problem-solving natures, then we
have got to have morals, consciences, personal difficulties to puzzle over, and to seek relief from them by
wreaking our will upon inanimate objects outside our
heads."

"We shall be so miserable," I said, "that we shall
give up and do nothing. Happiness is what makes
you interested in life."

"Not a bit of it," said Father cheerfully. "Makes

you slack. You will turn from your private tribulations to your work, and put new drive into it."

"I don't believe it," I said.

"You will in time," Father said. "And you must see the sense of not fighting over your sisters and aunts. With all this fire about, man's moral sense is in danger of falling behind his technological powers."

"That's a rotten argument," I said.

"I suspect it's one that we are going to hear with growing frequency."

"I mean," I said, "it contradicts the previous argument. First you say we need sexual morality in order to generate technological progress, and now you say we need sexual morality to be able to control technological progress. Which do you mean?"

"Both," said Father. "Alternative hypotheses. A perfectly respectable scientific approach to a problem. Either way you do what I tell you."

"Meanwhile, Father," I said sarcastically, "while we go off into the wilds to be exogamous and civilized, you have all the women at home to yourself. What is that, I should like to know, but the age-old picture of the primitive horde-father jealous of his growing sons?"

"Oh, come, come, Ernest," said Father deprecatingly. "That is quite uncalled-for. I have been a most indulgent parent. I *could* have been the heavy horde-father and thrown you out neck and crop. But instead I have brought you within smelling distance of—ah—a bevy of the most delightful girls. Besides, nobody could call *me* uxorious. I have always found women pall very quickly. There is a sameness about them; nudes in the mass are awfully boring. Not that I'm saying a word against your dear mothers; not a word. But my interests are really scientific."

"Father," said Alexander, who had been silent until now. "Father, just how do we get these girls from over the way?"

"You court them," said Father, and then added doubtfully, "I suppose. something like animals do. Blow out your chests like pigeons or your cheeks like bull-frogs or turn your bottoms orange or something."

"But I can't," said Alexander. "Anyway, I should feel too shy."

"Well, there you are then!" said Father. "You'll have to find out. Something for you to do for yourselves. Something to begin on. You don't expect me to solve *all* your difficulties, do you? When you're all happily mated, you can bring the girls home. We shall have a tribe then, instead of a mere horde. Now run along. And Oswald, don't try to track me. I know all your tricks; they're good, but I've been at the game for forty years and sure as Hoplophoneus was a cat if you do I'll put this spear through your midriff. Get going."

CHAPTER 10

I suppose we could have rushed Father if we had wanted. But he would certainly have got one of us, and probably two, before we got him. So, snarling and cursing, we backed away, while he shook his mighty spear at us. Then, out of range, we turned and slunk off southwards.

After we had gone some miles, however, Oswald called us to a halt. He was now our accepted leader.

"Listen, brothers," he said, "it's no use blundering along any old how. We've got to talk, to make a plan of attack. Blast the old man! We've got to go through with it. As I smell 'em, these people don't live more than fifteen or twenty miles from where we are now. We don't know what they're like, or what they're up to. We might run into a hunting party, and they might mistake us for a party of baboons and give us the works."

"Surely not!" protested Wilbur.

"Depends on which of us they saw first," growled his brother. "No sense in taking risks."

"If they're anything like us, they spear first and ask questions afterwards," I said. "You are right, brother. We must approach them with every care. What do you suggest?"

"We must arm ourselves, that is the first step," said Oswald incisively. "The old man's got our spears. Wilbur, that's your job. Find some flints and make axes and scrapers, so that we can sharpen spears. We'll look round for some likely timber for spears and clubs."

"But why must we make spears and clubs?" asked Alexander. "Why shouldn't we just go to them and explain why we're here? We're courting, not hunting."

"It's the same thing," said Oswald.

"Of course it is," I said. "We must get as near as we can unseen, and look the horde over. There are only four of us, and there may be forty of them. Our job is to track them, and then to cut off stragglers if they're on the move; or pounce on them at night, and each carry off a girl, like hyaenas."

Oswald nodded. "I agree with Ernest. You don't suppose they want to lose their women, do you? They have not got this crazy idea that they can't mate among themselves. They won't like what we're going to do to them one bit."

Alexander grumbled, "Well, I think it's a very crude way of gaining a girl's affection," but he put his shoulders as usual behind our preparations. As these were going forward, however, he suddenly said: "I say, you fellows, have you considered if—well, if the girls will like us?"

"They'll like us all right," said Oswald grimly, as he trimmed the knob of a three-foot shillelagh.

At last we were fully equipped and could begin to go forward again. We advanced cautiously against the wind, so that we might not easily be scented, and we did not close in until night fell. Then we found a spot to encamp. At dawn we moved up under cover of the mist and ensconced ourselves on a low cliff which we had already marked as giving us a commanding view of the place where the horde lived. As the mist began to disperse, we found that we were, indeed, looking almost directly down on them.

They lived on the shore of one of the brimming

lakes which water Africa in a well-nigh unbroken chain from Ethiopia to the Zambesi. Its grey-blue immensity stretched to the horizon, flanked by a series of volcanoes, from whose tops smoke rose unceasingly into the pale blue pall of the sky. But no smoke threw them back a challenge from the settlement below us. A promontory flanked by swamps thick with papyrus and elephant grass was pocked with holes scooped in the gravel, some of which were poorly roofed with the fronds of palm and bamboo. Here and there brown figures crouched among them; only the chip-chip of flint on flint proclaimed them for ape-men and not a company of chimpanzees.

"No fire; no cave," said Oswald, disgusted.

"And no idea what to do with a flint; just listen!" exclaimed Wilbur.

"And this is the class we're expected to mate into," I growled; "natural selection my thumb!" My bitterness against Father welled up in me again.

As the light increased, the sordidness of this palaeolithic slum became clearer; but Alexander said: "I'm not sure that it's quite as bad as you think. I rather like that girl." And indeed we could all see that an undeniably shapely girl had crawled from under one of the canopies and had gone down to the lakeshore to drink.

"Phacophaerus! You're dead right!" exclaimed Oswald with sudden enthusiasm. "She's got the hindquarters of a hippopotamus! Superb! Well, who'd have thought it in a dump like this?"

"There's another!" said Alexander in a delighted whisper, and he was right. A second splendid young rustic beauty had emerged into view and stood stretching her arms and thrusting out her bust as she took deep breaths of the morning air. As she oscillated down to the waterside she was followed by yet another magnificent female of the species, one of such elephantine proportions that Oswald smothered the wolf-whistle which began to issue from between Wilbur's lips only just in time.

"Control yourself, you lemur," snarled Oswald, though his own eyes were positively devouring the girl.

"Why, what are we waiting for?" demanded Wilbur. "Let's go down and get us one each."

"That's what," said Oswald pointing; and we then descried an unquestionably paternal figure, subhuman, indeed, in general outline, but gorilla-like in breadth of shoulder and muscular development, which restlessly patrolled the base of the promontory, mighty club in hand, and ever and anon lifted its widely flared nostrils to the light breeze, and even at that distance could be heard to emit grunts and growls which could only have one significance: followers were not allowed.

"I see," said Wilbur, and indeed our ardour cooled remarkably as we surveyed that menacing sentinel.

"A frontal attack would be far too costly," said Oswald. "Let's get back a bit where we can talk things over."

We withdrew to hold a council of war. "I vote for the night attack," said Oswald. "We'll go in after dark, roaring like lions, each grab a girl, and make off with her before the old boy knows what's up. How's that for a plan?"

I thought for a moment. "I expect he sleeps with one eye open, you know. Ought to, with all those lovely girls about. Besides, the girls may have brothers who stand guard, and who would raise the alarm when they heard lions coming. Even if we got through, in the darkness we shouldn't see who we were carrying off. I suppose it is those girls, not just any old women we're after?"

My brothers all nodded vigorously. "No, no, it won't do," said Alexander.

"Well, you suggest something," snapped Oswald.

"I suppose we couldn't carry torches?" Alexander hazarded.

"Yes, that's an idea," said Oswald. "That really might do the trick. They'd be just as terrified of fire as any other animal. We'd rush in with blazing brands in our hands, choose the girls we want by the light of them, and be gone before the horde had recovered from its panic."

I shook my head. "No, it still won't do. The nearest volcano is thirty miles from here, and they'd be sure to spot us carrying our torches long before we got anywhere near the place. We should lose all element of surprise, and even if they were frightened and ran away, the girls would run with them."

"All right," said Oswald. "That squashes that. Now you suggest something, Ernest—if you can. Looks to me as if we aren't going to get any girls the way you fellows crab everything."

But I had been thinking, and a plan had formed in my mind. "I think there's a simpler way to go about it," I said slowly. "Consider: they have no fire, so they can't do much big-game hunting. They are food-gatherers much more than hunters. That means that they have to range pretty far to get enough for the horde to eat. And *that* means it is ten to one the young women go out with the rest of them to catch rabbits and bush-babies and insects and suchlike while the males try for antelope. I expect they scatter widely. I propose that we divide up the country here-abouts into four territories and each of us takes one. Then, when a party enters the territory of one of us, it is up to him to track it, wait till he can cut a girl out, capture her and carry her off. They'll miss her, of course, but they'll put it down to leopards, like as not. They must lose their young in that way quite frequently. Of course, one of us may be unlucky, but we spread the risk by dividing up. I suggest we give each other a month, say, to get a girl, and then we all meet a month today at the place where we left Father, and join up to go home. With any decent luck, we'll all win through, and we'll get a girl each."

The others thought my plan over; and after some further discussion it was accepted as the most practical in the circumstances. We had, after all, surprise on our side; the horde would not have the faintest suspicion of what we were up to, since this kind of mating had been never been thought of before. There was a real chance that we would all get clean away with our loot.

And that was how I met Griselda.

CHAPTER 11

ello," she said. "You *do* look hot!"

I was hot. It seemed to me that I had chased that detestable girl through the length and breadth of Africa. My plan had worked perfectly. We had divided up the country behind the lake and each, like a spider in his web, had retired to his allotted place to await his prey. As I expected, the horde had straggled forth in search of provender, some to gather crocodiles' eggs, some to raid anthills for mongoose, some to dig for moles, some to chase monkeys and duikers and suchlike small game; and the girls had gone too. I tracked a party which entered my territory; I waited my chance until a girl became separated from it; I worked my way between her and it; I closed slowly upon her, growling like a leopard, and drove her farther inland; then, when she was too far from her relatives to summon aid, I charged. I expected to run her down, or tree her, easily. But I was wrong. When I reached the spot where I expected to make my kill, she wasn't there. She was about a hundred yards farther on, and I was slightly puffed.

However, I reckoned that if she had the better of me (not being a leopard) in a sprint, I should be able to wear her down in a long chase; and I settled down to do so. My only anxiety was whether she would be able to circle back to her starting point; but every time she showed any sign of so doing, by tremendous exertions I headed her off. Unfortunately, she always tried to circle back when this involved me in a rapid oblique movement through a swamp. She seemed to know which were the muddier, nastier and most leech-ridden swamps. But I was not going to be put off by gambits of that kind; I showed her that if it wasn't a leopard that was after her, it was a hippo. When I emerged from the swamps, coated with mud and leeches from head to foot, she would give me a run through the long grass, moving at the pace and with the stamina of an ostrich; and like an ostrich she seemed to be immune from the ticks which attached themselves to me. But I kept her waggling tailfeathers in view; I clung to her spoor; I refused to let her throw me off her scent.

Then she tried to confuse me by crossing water. I found that besides being able to run like an ostrich, she could swim faster than a crocodile. When she crossed rivers or lakes she kept just ahead of the crocodiles, whom she wakened from slumber by splashing like an unwary gibbon who has fallen from a branch and is being carried downstream. When I plunged in, the crocodiles already had plenty of way on, and, failing to catch her, could conveniently tack back for me. I invented a new fast crawl there and then, of which I should have been proud if I'd had time to think about it.

She tried to confuse the pursuit by dashing in among basking lions or sabre-toothed tigresses nursing their cubs. She usually did this when she was near a very tall tree, but I was a long way from one. Several nights we spent in trees not two hundred yards apart, and I made sure that when the lions had got tired of waiting I should catch her; but she was always down and away before I was.

She climbed several mountains. I gained on her as we made the ascent, and had it not been for the stones which, in her desperate attempts to escape, she dislodged with her feet, and which hit me on the head as I came up beneath her—usually when doing a difficult traverse—I would have caught her. But on the descent, she outdistanced me again; possibly because I had a headache.

Because she was ahead all the time she was, of course, able to catch the hyrax, the hare, and the squirrel as she sped; so she breakfasted and dined; by the time I came up all the game had been scared away; I had to make do on such indigestible scraps as she threw away. When I was not famished I had stomach-ache.

I asked myself, from time to time, if she was really worth it. On more than one occasion I decided she was not, and slowed down. What did I want with a mate anyway? I found, on examining my feelings, that after all I was perfectly indifferent. Perhaps the true value of the experience was to show me that I was cut out for bachelordom. But then the girl would suddenly spring from some bushes not twenty yards off, with a despairing scream, and the chance to swat her seemed too good to miss and, shillelagh upraised, on I would go again. But always by some skilful dodging she got away.

My pace gradually slowed to a walk. There was

no sprint in me, even when she showed herself on the skyline or seemed caught up in the jungle creepers almost under my hand. I was fed up with the whole thing. If Oswald could catch one of these women I would acknowledge him as the better man. I would call the courtship business off and rejoin the others at the rendezvous.

I had just made this decision when I blundered into a glade in the forest and there, seated on a fallen tree-trunk and casually combing her long, tawny hair with the backbone of a fish, Griselda smiled at me.

"You do look hot . . . and bothered."

"I've got you now," I said dispiritedly and raised my shillelagh.

She patted the tree-trunk. "Come and sit beside me and tell me all about yourself. I'm simply dying to know."

There seemed nothing else to do, and anyway my knees were aching with fatigue. I sat down and she took my shillelagh and propped it up beside us. I wiped my forehead with a tuft of star-grass.

"Whew!" I said.

"What's your name?" she asked, in a soft, encouraging voice.

"Ernest."

"That's a nice name. Sort of suits you. You're so

worried and serious-looking. Mine's Griselda. Silly, really, but my parents have awfully romantic ideas. So have I. Are you romantic?"

"No," I said.

"Oh, you must be, to hunt me for so long. Poor little me. I couldn't shake you off, simply could not. But I did my best, you must admit. I've been on the run for ten whole days."

"Eleven," I said. "Nearly twelve."

"Really?" said Griselda carelessly. "How time flies when one is *interested,* doesn't it? Did you enjoy the chase?" Her large brown eyes, like smooth pools beneath which crocodiles lie in wait were fastened questioningly upon my face.

"Er—very much," I said.

"That's all right then," she said. "I somehow knew we should get on, Ernest."

"Oh, did you?"

She clasped her hands and her feet. "From the very first day I got wind of you. I thought, what an *interesting* person; so unusual, so—well, so *different.*"

Rather against my will I was curious. "When was that, Griselda?"

"Why, the day you arrived, of course. You and your brothers. You all climbed up that hill and ogled us. It *was* rather rude. Father was frightfully angry.

Said the modern generation had no manners. Told us we were on no account to speak to any of you. Said he had a few words to say to you first."

"So you knew all about it," I said heavily. "Saw us and winded us."

"That's because you were so different," Griselda said quickly. "So distinctive." She lowered her voice and said softly: "So distinguished."

"And did you—did you guess what we had come for?"

"More or less," she said. "It was a bit obvious, wasn't it? We—my sisters and I—were *thrilled*."

"Oh, you were, were you?"

"Definitely. We don't meet many people where we live. It's a dull place." She pouted. "Father practically never lets us entertain. Or if he does, well—"

"Just so," I said. "He put us off, rather."

"We thought he might. So, you see, it was rather a problem. Luckily he had a bad accident with a rhinoceros not long ago. A head-on collision, you know; very careless of them both; they weren't looking where they were going. It has impaired Father's sense of smell, and he's got a slight astigmatism too."

"And the rhinoceros?"

"We ate it. Well, Father told us we must all stay at home and live on fish and eels until he had hunted you down; but we persuaded him that you had run away. He's rather vain about his appearance, though quite a *dear* when you know him properly. So then we just went out hunting as usual. And then you found me and chased me *mercilessly* and here I am!" She cast down her eyes submissively.

"Griselda," I said. "Let's get this absolutely straight. Do I understand that you deceived your horde-father and went out hunting knowing perfectly well that I would be waiting for you?"

"Well, I didn't know *exactly*, but I thought—"

"And when I grunted like lions and hippopotamuses you knew all the time it wasn't lions or hippopotamuses but me?"

"I think I would know your voice anywhere, Ernest; it's so—so *distinctive*, so—"

"And then," I went on, "not being in the least afraid—"

"I was *petrified*!"

"Not being in the least afraid," I shouted, "when I gave chase you deliberately ran for all you were worth through swamps and rivers and impenetrable jungle and up and down mountains like a cross between a duck and an ostrich and a goat—"

"Oh, darling, what a *sweet* thing to say!"

"And all the time you were simply leading me on

and had no real intention of getting away from me at all?"

"Of course not!"

I stared at her, speechless with fury.

"My dear," she protested. "A girl has her modesty, you know."

"Modesty! *You*—"

"Of course," she said, with dignity. "Besides, I thought you were enjoying it. I wanted to please you by giving you a good run."

"Please me!" I stormed. "A good run! I might have been killed a dozen times—"

"Oh, I don't think so, Ernest. You're so awfully strong. And so ardent, to chase me all that way. I could hardly wait to be caught, really."

"I don't believe a word of it," I fumed. "You have led me down the jungle path. You have made a monkey out of me! A regular long-tailed colobus monkey! You're a beastly girl. I can't think what I ever smelt in you! I'll have nothing more to do with you, do you hear? Nothing. I hate you."

Griselda's big brown eyes slowly filled with tears.

"I—only—tried—to—be—nice—to—you—"

I got up.

"I'm off," I snarled. "You can find your own way back. I won't capture you."

Blindly she stretched out her hand.

"Oh, but—but you have captured me! You can't go now. We're mates."

I was staggered by this idea.

"I have *not* captured you, Griselda. We are *not* mates! I'm going, I tell you!"

"You can't. It would be *too* dishonourable. It's—it's breach of promise. To chase me all this way and then just send me back, like a used-up flint core. I can't go home now. I'd rather die. If—if you leave, I will die. You've captured me and you must keep me."

"Rot!" I said, but I felt strange and upset inside. "I'm going and I'm not coming back. Good-bye."

I waited for her to say something—to admit that she was not captured and would go home. But she just sobbed.

I marched off furiously into the forest. I quite forgot my shillelagh.

CHAPTER 12

Night was already falling, but I was too incensed to notice. Griselda! She had proved to be a designing little minx, deceitful, shameless, and —yes—downright cruel. Malicious and unreasonable. The sheer effrontery of her last appeal took my breath away. Captured, indeed! And then to dissolve into womanly tears simply to get from pity what she had failed to encompass by the manoeuvres of a lioness in rut. Disgraceful. Could I even think of making such a woman the mother of my children?

Admittedly she was fast on her feet. She had outrun me, a male—though of course she had taken unfair advantage all the time. Still, I could hardly complain about that. Running away was running away: we all had to do it upon occasion, it was an art in itself, and Griselda had shown herself adept in its finer points. She would, undoubtedly, be able to teach them to her children, who would, in consequence, be fitter to survive.

There was something, too, in her point about not being able to go home. Her old man was plainly as jealous as horde-fathers could be. He would not be at all pleased at the way she had been gallivanting through Kenya, Tanganyika and probably Nyasaland with a young cave-man in hot pursuit. Of course, she would not die even if she did not go back. She could run with a herd of giraffe if need be. Sooner or later she would fall in with some representative of *Homo spp.* and get captured properly.

Did I want that? It occurred to me that, after all, I had run after her a very long way. It was a pity, in a sense, to give up at the kill. Detestably as she had treated me, moreover, it was clear that she had a very high opinion of me. I could hardly doubt the genuineness of her frank admiration. I was something quite new to her. Something, too, in extenuation of her behaviour, ought to be put down to a bad upbringing. What chance had she ever had in those low nests by the lakeside to discover the usages of decent horde life? In our cave she might improve. For one thing, she would be put in awe of me when she found that I was able to control fire; she would find our entire family much above her. That would take the wilfulness out of her. Beaten she would have to be, hard and often, but if I was firm from the very beginning—if I went right back now and gave her the thrashing of her young life—

No, she was impossible. And then, what an admission it would be if I did go back; what an admission that I was in the wrong, that I *had* captured her, that we *were* mates, that she had won! No, a thousand times No! Of course, she was quite a pretty girl. The horde would have to admit that. Father would be put out of countenance. He kept Elsie from me, and now I should keep Griselda from him. Just the sort of high-spirited girl he liked, too. I'd give him exogamy!

I came to a stop. It was now quite dark and the moon had not yet risen. Immersed in my own thoughts I had not heeded the rising roar of the jungle traffic. Now it was in full cacophony. The frogs were hard at it, shouting each other down in the swamps; predacious flies whined through the air; the screeches of hyrax were answered by the screeches of owls; crocodiles and hippopotamuses grunted from the rivers; the leopards coughed in the undergrowth; and hyaenas laughed hysterically as they sprang up and down trees after screaming monkeys. Out in the clearings, lions put up game and the thud of twenty thousand hoof-beats shook the earth. Near at hand elephants trumpeted shrilly as trees came away in their trunks with a crackle of torn roots and the diverse screams of the rich fauna which inhabited their foliage. Everyone was after everyone else, determined to prove himself the dominant species; and I suddenly realized two things: first, that someone was after me, and second, that I had forgotten my shillelagh.

I turned and ran. Not even Griselda could have outstripped me. I tore through the jungle, hurdling bushes, leaping streams, swinging daringly through the air by the lianas which festooned the forest trees. Should I take refuge up a tree or not: that was the question. If it was a big cat, I would be safe; if it was a smaller cat it would follow me and then, on some swinging branch seventy feet above the ground, it would be only my teeth and hands against its teeth and claws. Yet if I stayed on the ground I should be run down; if I plunged into water, the crocodiles were waiting. I tore on, my heart bursting, my breath coming in choking sobs. I could feel my pursuer close behind. A clearing opened before me; it was, I knew, the end—the ideal place for it to spring on my back. But it was too late to stop. Momentum fairly carried me out into the moonlight, a perfect target; I heard the great cat pause, crouch and leave the ground; everything was red before my eyes as I made a last desperate, hopeless spurt; and then, just as I expected to feel a dozen talons sink into my flesh as a huge, hot-smelling weight hurled me to the ground, there came the most tremendous thwack! and the sound of a heavy body thudding to the earth behind me. It was as though the weight under which my shoulders were already bowing was lifted clear of me; but it was a few seconds before I could slow down and look over my shoulder. When I did, it was to see a leopard sprawling in the grass, and an ape-man running to-wards it, whirling my bloodstained shillelagh aloft. Thwack! Crunch! The leopard's brains were expertly beaten out before he could recover from the stunning blow that had dropped him in the middle of his spring.

"Griselda!" I gasped.

"Ernest," she answered. "My darling! I knew you would come back to me! You *do* look hot. How hard you must have been running. Never mind, dinner's ready. Let's start at once, shall we?"

I should, of course, have given her that thrashing

there and then; but I was badly puffed, and hungry too; and she had the shillelagh anyway. I decided to postpone endearments until we had forestalled the jackals and hyaenas which would soon scent the leopard's sudden demise. A heavy meal on top of my exertions, however, disposed me inexorably to sleep, and I sank down exhausted at the foot of a mimosa tree, Griselda standing guard with the shillelagh.

I woke refreshed a few hours later. The moon was sinking behind the mountains, but everything was tinted with silver. Griselda was sitting on the log gazing pensively at the last vulture that was picking over the leopard's silver bones. But what brought me to my feet with a leap was the way she had done up her long hair round the leopard's jaw-bone, and the artful way the leopard's tail was looped round her neck and hung down between her breasts in consummate coquetry.

"Griselda!" I cried in a voice of thunder. "I've got you now!"

CHAPTER 13

Love! Sweet love! I shall always maintain that it was one of the very greatest discoveries of the Middle Pleistocene, rich and fertile as that period was in invention and cultural development. At the time it took me totally by surprise. I was suddenly as new a creature as a snake that has sloughed its skin, free, flexible, aerated with delight. I was a dragonfly on the wing after the long night in the chrysalis. These are banal, worn-out metaphors now; the modern generation has missed that first, fine, careless rapture. Young people today know what to expect; they have been told too much; they anticipate too ambitiously.

But to me it was a metamorphosis just because I had no inkling of what I was to go through. Yes, there is a special privilege in being the very first to undergo a new human experience, whatever it may be; and for that to be love! Think of it! Love, humbly pleased as the young still seem to be with it when they find it in the jungle or by the lakeside or on a mountain peak, is now a second-hand, humdrum affair which has taken its place usefully in the evolutionary process; but oh! when it was new-born!

I had no power or wish to analyse the thing; looking back, I perceive it sprang, an unpremeditated fruit, from that first inhibition which Father laid on us for purely sociological purposes. Our easy inclinations were pruned back, and this luscious, enthralling, extraordinary banquet of sensations was the unsought bounty. Not that we were inhibited, Griselda and I, as we paraded the world together. On the contrary, we not only felt absolute in the new dominions within ourselves, but treated all nature as the appurtenances of our nuptial chamber. We felt invulnerable; as though the union of two flimsy, thin-skinned half-creatures had made an invincible master for the earth.

We laughed irreverently in the haunts of the lions; we darted upon the sleeping cheetah and twisted his tail; we chased each other across the shallow waters using the backs of dumbfounded crocodiles and mystified hippopotamuses as stepping-stones; we leapt up the waterfalls with the perch and tiger-fish and shot the rapids with the eels. We played tag with the egrets beneath the legs of outraged elephants who stamped too late and trumpeted in vain; we cast quoits of bougainvillaea and morning glory over the horns of disgusted rhinoceroses; we stampeded the deer from their pasture with well-aimed streamers of jasmine and rubber-vine which flew like pennons in the wind from their tossing antlers. We joined hands with the monkeys before they knew we were among them and whirled them round in a ring-a-ring-a-frangipani. From ostrich, flamingo, firebird and a hundred others I snatched enamelled feathers for Griselda's hair; and I wore on my head an aepyornis's egg for a solar topi. Our peals of delighted laughter resounded through the bush and between the vine-strung trees; the great lakes rippled it to the mountains and the mountains echoed it back to the plains.

It was the most colossal fun, though we nearly overstepped the mark once or twice.

After sundown we strolled forth, arms twined round each other's waists, to enjoy the bright lights; the glittering stars continuously shot through by lavish displays of meteorites, the flames that belched from the mountains round the horizons, the gleam of cats' eyes in the undergrowth, the ceaseless sparkle of fireflies about our feet. Then I told Griselda of the cave I was going to take her to; of the great fire that burned ceaselessly at its entrance, and the great row that blew up if anyone let it go out; of our prowess with spear and trap and the great feasts we had. In her turn she was never tired of cross-questioning me about her new in-laws, and spoke piteously of the tyranny from which I had rescued her; a straitlaced, domineering sire who exacted utter submission from his terrorized women-folk and who was even then preparing to expel his growing sons from the horde. Her eyes were bright as any hawk's when she exclaimed:

"Oh, Ernest, I *am* going to enjoy myself!"

Oh, love!

CHAPTER 14

Suddenly our honeymoon was over, and it was time to make for the place which I had chosen for the reunion with my brothers and their mates—if they had caught any. Oswald, I was sure, would be successful, but I had my doubts about Wilbur and Alexander. Griselda, however, professed no doubts at all that her three sisters would, as she expressed it, have "got themselves off." She suggested that we should approach the rendezvous secretly, see who arrived there first, and who had got whom.

Only Oswald had arrived, and sure enough sat by

the lake talking with a fine, plump girl who hung on his words with parted lips and shining eyes.

"That prune Clementina!" giggled Griselda.

"So there I was, entirely alone," Oswald was saying; "not a tree in sight, my spear broken, even the wounded lion running for his life, as the buffalo charged. There was only one thing to do, and I did it. I ran towards him as fast as I could go, put my hands on his horns and vaulted over him so quickly that he had no time even to toss his head."

"Oswald, how *terrifying*!" gasped the girl.

"Another time," Oswald began, when we broke cover and charged them both with shouts of joy.

Presently, after we had congratulated each other on our prizes, and the girls had gone off to find us something to eat, I asked Oswald how his courtship had gone. He laughed. "Easy as falling off a crocodile, my dear chap," he said. "Mind you, she gave me a bit of a run. Well! A girl's got her modesty, you know!"

"How—er—how long a run, Oswald?" I asked.

"Oh, I don't know," he said carelessly. "About a fortnight, perhaps. She's got a fair turn of speed, has Clemmie, and then, I was carrying my shillelagh. I enjoyed every minute of it."

"Climb any decent mountains?" I asked casually.

"One or two, one or two," said Oswald, putting his hand up to the back of his head for a moment. "Playful kitten, Clemmie. How did you get on, Ernest?"

"Much the same, much the same," I said. "But it looks as if Alexander and Wilbur are—er—still hunting, doesn't it?"

Oswald nodded soberly. "I rather wonder," he said, "if there's much point in waiting for them. Frankly it wouldn't surprise me if they were a year or two on the job."

But at that very moment we were startled by a tremendous crashing in the undergrowth, as though some ungainly animal such as a warthog, antlion or armadillo were approaching; it was, however, Wilbur and another girl who, blinded with sweat and bowed like chimpanzees, staggered into view, each carrying an enormous red rock.

"Honoria, darling!" screamed Griselda and Clementina, as the new girl dropped her burden with a thump, and in a trice the three were chattering like parrots.

"Wilbur," said Oswald, "what on earth do you think you are doing?"

Wilbur put down his rock with care beside his mate's and straightened up with an effort.

"Oh, hello, you chaps," he said. "Hot, isn't it?"

"What have you got there?" I said.

Wilbur grinned. "Jolly interesting. Never noticed this formation before. Been experimenting with it. I think Father's going to find it's got remarkable possibilities."

"You mean you're going to carry that dunnage all the way home? For pity's sake! How far have you lugged it?"

"Oh, a goodish way. You don't find it in our parts, as far as I can see. Result of weathering, I fancy; basically it's some volcanic dust compound. Honoria helped me. Good girl, must introduce you—Honoria!"

"You don't mean to tell me," said Oswald, eyeing Honoria's muscular limbs, "that you chased this girl carrying half a mountain with you?"

"He didn't chase me at all!" said Honoria in a discontented tone. "Though I tried to attract his attention ever so. He kept messing about with these beastly stones and didn't take the least notice of me. I went right up to him and said, 'Busy, aren't you?' and guess what he said! 'I am, rather.' That's what he said. Just like that. 'I am, rather.'"

"Coo!" said Griselda. "What did you do then, darling?"

"I said, 'What do you call yourself, Mr. Busy? A geologist or something?' And what do you think he said?"

"Oh, go *on,* darling," hissed Griselda.

"He said, 'Only an amateur, I'm afraid,' just like that: 'Only an amateur.' Well, I nearly walked off. I would have, too; but then he said, 'I say, just give me a hand with this bit, will you; it's coming loose,' and I could see he wouldn't even *look* at me till he'd got his toy, so I thought I'd better, and I did, and the stone came right away in my hand and fell on Mr Amateur Geologist's toes, with not half of a bump, and then he *couldn't* chase me, even if he'd wanted to, but stood on one foot like a stork and hooted like a hornbill."

Wilbur looked sheepish. "I must say, Honoria was a flint. She stuck around keeping lions and leopards away until I could walk again, and then helped me enormously in my work."

"Oh, enormously!" exclaimed Honoria.

"And so we're mates," concluded Wilbur simply.

"So are *we,*" said a shy voice behind us. We all spun round and there was Alexander, with his shillelagh in the crook of one arm and a really lovely girl, the one that had the amplitudes of a hippopotamus, clinging fondly to the other.

"Alex!" "Petronella!" we cried, and the round of introductions and congratulations was gone through once more.

As soon as we could, however, Oswald, Wilbur and I drew Alexander aside and asked him how he had won the favour of the fair Petronella; there was no question but that she absolutely doted on him.

He looked rather surprised. "Well the usual thing, I suppose. The day after we parted I was hidden in a thicket watching ducks—amazing things they are, too—when suddenly they all took off in a lather of foam—takes them about three feet to get airborne, by the way—when Petronella passed right in front of me. I leapt up and knocked her senseless with one blow of my shillelagh. That was right, wasn't it?" he added anxiously.

"Perfectly right," said Oswald, his face a study.

"Oh, good," said Alexander with relief. "I thought it a bit crude. She had rather a sore head when she came to, poor dear, but I soon had her laughing over some sketches of ducks which I'd done on a spit of sand to pass the time while she was unconscious. We had a beautiful honeymoon," he said with a happy smile. "Really beautiful. Isn't love wonderful?"

"Isn't it!" we chorused.

A few days later we set off for home. It was rather

a slow journey as Wilbur could not be parted from his rocks. He and Honoria would stagger about ten yards with them and then have to put them down. Honoria several times suggested that her sisters should help, but they invariably replied, "He's your mate, dear."

So we had plenty of time for hunting trips, sightseeing, picnics, bird-watching and even art appreciation on the way. At last, however, we reached familiar country and had to go carefully to avoid booby-traps. Presently we descried a long spiral of smoke that rose high into the sky, and the girls' astonishment was unbounded. They simply could not believe that it was industrial smoke, not volcanic. But as we got nearer, we began to look at each other uneasily. Something was wrong. I sensed it. Oswald sensed it. Alexander, the girls, even Wilbur, panting hard and bent double, became aware of it. At last Oswald spoke for us all.

"What is that appalling stench?"

CHAPTER 15

We stood and sniffed. "It reminds me of something," I said, "but I can't place it."

"It's not corpses, and it's not volcanoes," said Oswald, "but something is burning. I am afraid there has been an accident."

"I don't find it altogether unpleasant, though," said Alexander. "It's having a curious effect on me: my mouth is watering."

We discovered that it was having this effect on everybody.

"Come on," said Oswald. "We had better see," and, with Wilbur and Honoria laboriously bringing up the rear, we hurried forward to the cave, the strange, tantalizing but piquant smell increasing all the time.

The entire horde, we saw with relief, was at home and sitting round the fire, which was, however, spitting, sizzling and crackling in a most extraordinary manner. Every now and then an aunt rose, stuck a green stick into the embers and drew it forth again with a chunk of burning material on the end.

"Why, that's a shoulder of horse," gasped Oswald.

"And that's a loin of antelope," I replied. We took the last mile at a run, and, with our mates hotfoot behind us, burst into the family circle.

"Welcome home, my dears," shouted Father, starting up.

"Just in time for dinner," cried Mother, and there were tears of joy on her dear, soot-streaked face. Then there was such a shouting, hugging, sniffing, embracing and laughing. "Clementina? Oswald *is* a lucky man!" "And who is Miss Bright Eyes? Griselda? *Just* what Ernest needs, my dear!" "Petronella? but her figure is *superb*—who'd have thought our Alexander could get a girl like that to look at him!" "And Honoria? Well, well, how nice—and what is this you have brought us? A lovely big rock?

But how *thoughtful* of you, dear, to bring us *anything*," and so on, until I made my voice heard.

"Mother! Why on earth are you using good meat for firewood?"

"Oh, Ernest, I quite forgot my joint in all the excitement; I'm afraid it will be dreadfully overdone—" and she hastily disengaged herself from the mêlée and pulled a great, smoking hunk of antelope from the fire.

"Oh, dear," she said, inspecting it. "This side is burnt to cinders."

"Never mind, my love," said Father. "You know I like a bit of crackling. I'll take the outside with pleasure."

"But what are you talking about?" I implored them.

"Talking about? Cooking, of course!"

"What's cooking?" I inquired patiently.

"The dinner," said Father. "Oh, of course, now I come to think of it, your mother hadn't invented it before you boys went away. Cooking, my sons, is— well—is a way of preparing game before you eat it; it's an entirely novel method of reducing—er—ligaments and muscles to a more friable form for mastication—and—er—"

He frowned, and then a happy smile broke on his face. "But after all, why am I trying to explain it? The proof of the roast is in the eating. Just try some and see."

My brothers and our mates were crowding round the strange, aromatic piece of meat which Mother now proffered to us. The girls, who had already shied at the fire, backed timidly away; but Oswald boldly seized the joint, raised it to his muzzle, sank his teeth into it and tore away a piece. Immediately his face went crimson; he spluttered, choked, gasped, swallowed violently, dropped the joint (which Mother neatly caught) and writhed in agony; water ran out of his eyes and he madly pawed his mouth and throat.

"Oh, sorry, Oswald," said Father. "Of course, you didn't know. I ought to have mentioned it's hot."

"Run to the river, dear," said Mother, "and drink some water."

In a flash Oswald had vanished and a moment later came the sound of a tremendous splash.

"We're used to it now," Father said to me, "but to start with, you must go carefully. A good plan is to begin by blowing on it; then nibble the edges a bit, and you'll get the hang of the thing in no time."

Thus warned, the rest of us set to work to practise the new cuisine. We burned our mouths at first, but we found it was worth persevering. The meat seemed literally to melt in the mouth; the taste—the mingled flavour of cinder, wood ash and half-burned meat, the lean tenderized, the fat semi-liquescent—was ambrosial. Especially the red gravy! Practically no serious chewing was required; the built-in strength and elasticity of striped muscle that would drive a 500-pound gnu at 50 mph positively dissolved on the tongue. It was a revelation.

We begged Mother to tell us how she had made this pivotal discovery. But she only smiled, and it was William who said, half sulkily, half in pride, "It was my poor little piggy-wig!"

Father explained. "Yes, William has his share in this remarkable invention, the possibilities of which we have, I fancy, yet barely sniffed at. You remember the dog? Well, William tried the experiment again, soon after you went a-courting, this time with a young boar, which he called Piggy. I have rarely known a messier, smellier, stupider or more recalcitrant animal. William kept it on a lead of twisted rubber-vine, but even so, it was adept at butting people behind the knees. Or, if it did not do that, it would run round and round people until they were trussed up with its lead; then it bit them repeatedly. Well, one day we were all out hunting, except your mother and the toddlers, and it seems that Piggy had got himself trussed up to a large piece of firewood, and your mother somehow didn't notice this when she put the log on the fire."

"So she says," growled William.

"So Piggy got burnt to death," said Father. "But the brilliance of the thing was the way that your mother recognized that he was good to eat at a certain intermediate stage in the process of combustion, and pulled him out then, and only then. A remarkable example of intuitive thought cutting suddenly to the heart of a problem; an instantaneous synthesis of ideas which the brain of a mere ape would be wholly inadequate to—"

"But Mother," I asked, "what made you connect the burning pig with something good to eat?"

"Well, my dear," said Mother, "I suppose it was very silly really, but you know how bad Father's heartburn has been lately—especially after he's eaten elephant—and I was worrying about him; and then, as poor William's piggy began to frizzle I could not help remembering the funny smell when Uncle Vanya stood on the embers and Auntie Pam sat on them, and how very tender they found the places were which caught fire."

So that was why the smell of cooking had seemed

familiar to me! "Genius," said Father reverently. "Pure genius. And an incalculable step forward for the species as a whole. The possibilities are stupendous."

"Can you cook anything?" asked Oswald, "or only pig and antelope?"

"Anything," said Father expansively. "The bigger the animal, the bigger the fire, that's all. If you will bring in a mammoth, I will engage to build a fire large enough to cook him with."

"I'll do it," said Oswald.

"Do it, my dear boy," said Father, "and we will have a grande horde celebration. We ought to have one anyway—a tremendous blow-out, you know, with after-dinner speeches. Yes," he added thoughtfully, "I shall certainly make a speech."

Oswald immediately set about making plans for a hunting expedition on a most ambitious scale. I noticed that Father was now quite content to leave everything to Oswald. He and Wilbur were continually going off by themselves into the bush with a mysterious air; they refused to answer any questions and often came back late for meals. The women were settling down happily enough, in the way women and monkeys do: continually screeching and quarrelling and fondling and talking woman-talk—that specialized dialect in which every other word is italicized. But to my grief I found a change had come over my darling sister Elsie. I had looked forward, even on my honeymoon, to seeing her again, and had told Griselda all about her—who at once said, "I am sure I'm going to be *great* friends with Elsie." It had occurred to me that in due course, and whatever Father said, there was no reason why Elsie should not come and live with Griselda and me; I would start a really ambitious horde of my own. A harem—like the chimpanzees, and from the first, Elsie seemed to adore Griselda. They were constantly together, Griselda taught Elsie how to hang fragments of animal hide round her neck and to do up her hair with fishbones and orchids; Elsie taught Griselda how to cook. But Elsie had no time for me. All the comradely feeling which used to exist between us seemed to have vanished. If I went up to speak to her, she replied brusquely, "Don't bother me now, Ernest, can't you see I'm busy?" and if I gave her the grilled kidneys I found in my helping of roast lamb, she immediately passed them on to the younger children or to Griselda, saying, "These are yours, darling; you really *must* teach Ernest better table manners." This was harder to bear in that Elsie had now grown up to be a really lovely young woman, in curves and colour the perfect complement to Griselda, and just as fleet of foot and sure of eye.

Nor did I appreciate the way Father made much of the two girls. When he returned from his mysterious forays with Wilbur, sometimes tired and discouraged, he seemed to want only their company; and soon one would hear the three of them laughing happily together. More than once I caught Father strolling along, Griselda on one side and Elsie on the other, with an arm round the waist of both. Nor was he in the least abashed when I joined them. "Ah, Ernest," he cried. "Your old father can still get off with a brace of pretty girls, you see!"

"I thought your interests were purely scientific," I replied coldly, and marched off. For some reason they all seemed to find this exquisitely funny. When later I remonstrated with Griselda, she only said, rubbing noses with me: "Don't worry, you jealous old thing. I'm cultivating your family. But I love *you*, and I'm going to keep *you*." I was still miserable, however.

I found that regular cooked meals made a big difference to my life. Now that eating took so much less time, I had at last the leisure to put my thoughts in order. Oswald used the time saved to hunt, and Father to experiment; but I devoted a good deal of it to introspection. It then came almost as a shock to me to realize how much went on above my jaws and behind my eyes quite independently of what went on in front of them. So independently, in fact, that when I slept these inward events continued, and still more vividly; but I lost control of them entirely, and they became a sort of mirror-image, a still-water reflection, of the spatial world in which my outward limbs moved. Yet I had a body in that world too; a shadow body which sometimes flashed from point to point at a hundred miles an hour but seemed rooted to the ground when I desperately wanted to escape from a lion. It was not enough to dismiss all this as dreaming; for it was as solidly a part of reality as my flint axe. It happened. Unpredictable and frightening as was the outer world, still more unpredictable and frightening was the inner.

One night in dreamland, for example, I was hunted hour after hour by a lion. At last he cornered me; at bay I threw my spear—it seemed to have become the merest reed. Yet it flew lightly through the air and spitted the lion as easily as if he had been the roast gibbon I had had for supper; in an incomprehensible way, moreover, the lion *was* the gibbon. Whereupon the lion said cheerfully: "At last, Ernest, you have done something for the species! You have superseded the boss beast. The possibilities are stupendous. Properly exploited, they will carry subhumanity to the top branches of the tree of evolution. Glory, glory, alleluia, mine eyes behold the end of the Pleistocene!"

With Father's voice ringing in my ears, I woke beneath the stars, trembling and sweating. From that day to this I have never touched roast gibbon last thing at night.

CHAPTER 16

Oswald's preparations were now complete; one morning he returned from an extensive reconnaissance to tell us that large herds of mammoth, elephant, bison, buffalo and a fine selection of ungulates were moving into a good position for attack. The whole horde marched out within the hour, leaving Mother and Aunt Mildred in charge of the children of pre-hunting age. Oswald took command of the whole operation, and Father obeyed his orders with alacrity and smartness. Oswald spread the main body of his force through the country in a great net, into which the animals would walk upwind; a smaller detachment, mainly women, was to execute a forced march across country to get behind the herds and drive them by noise and shouting into the net; the smaller children acted as runners to inform him as each posse of hunters got into position. He himself, with his staff, climbed a hill conveniently placed to enable him to conduct operations, and to join any hunters who might need reinforcements at the kill.

Everything went off well. The herds were soon frightened by the beaters, and ran blindly into ambush after ambush. With great skill, some of Oswald's hunting parties drove mammoths and elephants into pits and booby-traps, while others with their spears picked off horses, zebras, buffaloes, elands and even gazelles in order that we might have a variety of meat. Within a week we had far more for the larder than we could carry home; but as usual we had to share our kill with a host of hyaenas, jackals, vultures and kites which flocked from every quarter to gorge themselves at our expense. "Well, well," said Father, surveying the carnage with satisfaction. "Remember the time when we were among the scavengers? Now they follow us," and with a well-aimed stone he sent a hyaena limping off with howls of disappointed rage.

Laden with meat of every kind we turned cheerfully homewards, and found Mother ready for us with a mighty fire. Soon we were fashioning skewers, spits and jacks from green wood; spreading embers for grills; heaping up wood ash to broil ostrich, aepyornis, stork and flamingo eggs. A mighty glare lit up the country round as night fell; and shortly afterwards Uncle Vanya arrived.

"Ah Vanya!" cried Father cheerily. "Just in time for the great celebration! Good of you to come!'

Uncle Vanya gazed glumly at the banquet which was cooking, sniffed its fascinating aroma, and said: "You're going from bad to worse, Edward. Have you considered what cooked food will do to your teeth? Half of you have got dental decay by now, I shouldn't wonder. Yes I'll stay. But it's a melancholy occasion for me, I can tell you."

However, he was prevailed upon to try the various dishes and as far as I could see made just as hearty a meal as anybody else.

And what a barbecue it was, served with more than Homeric culinary skill: every kind of meat roasted, grilled, basted, fried. For the main course we cut slices from the thighs of elephants, antelopes, and bison, wrapped them in folds of fat and laid more raw meat above them; when the thighs were oven-

hot we sprinkled the animals' blood, the juice of berries and the yolks of aepyornis eggs over them amid
the dancing flames; then we drew them out and con-
sumed the inner parts and cut up smaller pieces and
toasted them on spits.

At last we had finished. Then Father rose and
spoke.

"Kinsfolk, mates, sons and daughters! This is indeed a happy and auspicious occasion, and one which
I feel should not be allowed to pass without a few
words to mark its significance, to review past achieve-
ments and dedicate us to future tasks. Tonight we
officially welcome to the horde four charming young
ladies who have become the mates of our four eldest
young males. But we do more than that: for their
arrival here inaugurates the new custom whereby an
ape-man shall go forth and find his mate from another group in the subhuman family and an ape-girl
shall leave father and mother and cleave to her soul-
mate. This noble institution, as I have already explained, should generate new energy which will
surely find expression in speeding up the pace of
moral and material progress. I am quite certain that
those who have participated in this important experiment, painful as it was at first, feel enormously the
better for it."

"Hear, hear," said Oswald, Wilbur, Alexander and the girls, as Father paused for applause.

"Technologically," Father went on, after bowing his acknowledgement, "we are passing through a veritable revolution. The improvement of flint tools is slow, but it is steady. On the other hand, in the mastery of fire, we have now an invincible weapon in our march to world supremacy."

"Shame, oh, shame!" cried Uncle Vanya. "Wilbur, just see if you can split this thighbone for me, my dear boy, I can't get all the marrow out."

"Ah, I thought I should surprise you," Father said, "but surely it is obvious? Did you suppose when we threw the bears out of this cave that we should rest content with that? It was but one important battle in a great war. Every day ape-men are being killed and eaten by carnivores, squashed flat by elephants, mastodons and hippopotamuses, run through by rhinoceroses, tossed to their deaths by every animal that has horns, stung to death by every snake that has venom in its bite or squeezed to death by those that have not. And what fang, horn, hoof or venom leaves is destroyed by a host of other deadly foes, many so small as hardly to be seen, but coming in such countless hosts that they cannot be—as yet—defeated. Man's days on earth are few, and the very species is in constant peril of extinction. Our answer is defiance; to set ourselves to the extermination of every species that preys on us, to spare only those that submit. To every other species we cry: Beware! Either you shall be our slaves or you shall disappear from the surface of the earth. We will be master here; we will outfight, outthink, outmanoeuvre, outpropagate and outevolve you! That is our policy and there is no other."

"Yes there is," said Uncle Vanya. "Back to the trees."

"Bah! Back to the Miocene!" snapped Father.

"There was nothing wrong with the old Miocene," snarled Uncle Vanya. "People knew their place—"

"And look at them now: fossils!" retorted Father. "You can go back or you can go on; but you cannot sit still—even in the trees. I tell you an ape-man can have but one duty: to go on—to manhood, to history, to civilization! Let us, then, tonight, dedicate ourselves—"

Boom! Boom! Boom! Uncle Vanya began to beat his chest with his fists like a disdainful gorilla.

"Let us," said Father, raising his voice, "let us, I say, determine never to be satisfied, always to seek improvement. In the making of flints let us go forward from the Palaeolithic to the Neolithic—"

Wilbur with a shout clashed two flint cores to-gether, *chip, chip chip*!

"Let us, in the hunting field, steadily improve our missiles—"

Oswald began to clatter his spears fiercely together.

"On the home front, let the domestic arts free us ever more completely for the great struggle—"

Beaming at him Mother began to click between her fingers the little bones that she used to teach the babies how to cut their milk teeth.

"Let the fine arts grow and stimulate our observation of nature—"

Alexander seized a discarded ram's horn and blew a strange honk out of it.

"And let those who have contributed nothing much as yet to this great enterprise but wind and argument bestir their wits—"

I began to whistle derisively.

The noise was now tremendous, and entirely drowned the end of Father's speech. Uncle Vanya was beating his chest with a steady reverberation, and everybody else seemed to be banging or clattering something. Somehow Father's voice rose again above the uproar—"That's it, keep it up, we're really getting somewhere now! Presto, Oswald! Hold the note,

Ernest! Now bring in the percussion, Vanya, that's it, and you too, now, Wilbur. Now the wind, Alexander; castanets, my love, please; drums again, Vanya—"

Clatter, clash, rah-rah, boom-boom! Clash, clatter! Coo-ee rah-rah, boom-boom!

Stick in hand, Father was now pointing to us in order, beckoning us on or dampening us down with his other hand. The noise began to take a shape; to become alive, a patterned snake swinging from side to side, writhing round and back and in on itself.

Rah-boom-rah, clatter, clash! Coo-ee, clatter, rah-boom!

There was a stir and a movement beyond us. The women had risen to their feet and had begun to shuffle strangely to and fro, to and fro, pummelling the air with their fists and elbows.

"Keep it up!" yelled Father desperately, as the line of women swayed out into the firelight. "Hold the beat! Molto Allegro! Presto! drums! castanets! wind! Swing it!"

Down in the forest the lions roared their disapproval, the elephants trumpeted in shrill protest from the swamps and all the jackals in the jungle were set a-barking. Our days on earth might be few; the species thinly spread; the struggle for survival hard and the Palaeolithic Age stretching interminably before us; but we were dancing.

Sweat poured down our muzzles and our flanks as we banged away for dear life; Uncle Vanya had beaten himself black and blue; Father's voice was hoarse; but still the women swung to and fro and wheeled and whirled and howled in the firelight; what a dance that first dance was!

It ended abruptly. Into our midst hurtled half a dozen great shapes, pounced on the line of women, and amid screams and the flailing of legs swung high in the air, made off with them like eagles taking the prey. Elsie, Ann, Alice, Doreen were swept away into the darkness; and several aunts were taken too. Puffed as I was with whistling, I started in pursuit; but only to stumble unaccountably over Griselda's outstretched legs and fall flat on my face. Oswald hurled his spears in vain, Wilbur and Alexander stood nonplussed. Aunt Mildred had shot under Uncle Vanya's protecting arm like a bush-baby into its burrow; Father merely gazed with mild interest, his baton raised as though we were about to start the music again. As far as our sisters were concerned the rape was complete.

Half-stunned as I was, I tried to get together a party to go in pursuit.

"You leave my brothers alone, Ernest," said Griselda.

"Mating and giving in mateship," said Father. "Well, Mother, we've got the girls off our hands now. Don't cry; they are capital cooks and will make splendid wives; it's the way of the world, you know."

Enlightenment burst on me. I glared from Father to Griselda and back again. So that was what the precious pair of them—and Elsie too!—had been so thick about! Oh, the sickening perfidy of it!

"You planned it all!" I thundered.

"No, no, my boy," said Father. "Let's say I left it to nature—just pointing the way a bit, that's all."

"But they've left me!" wailed Aunt Pam. "They've taken Aggie and Angela and Nellie, and they've left me!" Indeed, she was the only widow aunt left.

"Well, they've not been long gone," said Father.

In a moment Aunt Pam, her long hair flying, had dashed into the darkness.

"Wait for me!" she shrieked, and her cries could be heard ever farther and fainter from the jungle. "Wait for me!"

CHAPTER 17

One afternoon not long afterwards, Father came bounding into the cave with Wilbur hard at his heels.

"We've done it!" he cried in a voice of delight. "Hurrah! Hurrah! We've *done* it!"

"Done what?" everyone exclaimed except me. Resignation in my voice I said, "What have you done *now*?"

"Come and see," shouted Father. "Don't tell them, Wilbur. Let them see for themselves. Come on, everybody. Everybody. It's too good to miss." In a body we followed Father and Wilbur into the bush for several miles and then climbed a hill.

"Look!" cried Father dramatically.

At the foot of the hill rose a long column of smoke, and we could hear the crackle of a big fire. "Another fire," we said.

"We made it," said Father, bursting with pride.

"You mean you've been up the volcano again, dear?" asked Mother. "That's extremely quick. You only went out this morning."

"We haven't been up the volcano," said Father. "We're never going up the damned volcano again. We made the fire! Made it from nothing. Or rather, from flints. That red stone that Wilbur brought from the lake: it's wonderful stuff. When you strike it with our ordinary flints, how the sparks fly! Not just one or two, but whole bursts of them. The thing was, to capture them. We tried everything until this morning we got the answer. Just a few dry leaves lightly powdered to chaff in the hand! Think of it! Just a few dry leaves, then a few dry twigs, then a small dry bit of wood, and so on. You must blow it up and build it up from an absolutely tiny beginning that hardly looks like a fire at all."

I saw the idea. "Well done," I said, nodding.

"Wherever we go now," Father said happily, "we can have a fire at will. You just take this new red stone with you—a mere flake will do—and a flint, and start it up when you want it. The possibilities are stupendous."

"The fire you made is getting pretty big, too," I said.

"Oh, we only made quite a small one," said Father. "It will go out in a minute. It doesn't matter, because we can start another when we like. Let's show them, Wilbur. It's nice and dry here."

"Before you start another," I said, "we'd better make sure that one goes out, hadn't we?"

But it was suddenly clear that the fire was not going out. On the contrary, even while Father had been speaking, it had grown tremendously. Smoke was now billowing upwards in great clouds and began to reach us. The children started coughing. A tremendous roar rolled up from the plain.

"I expect it will go down in a moment," said Father uneasily. "We only left a couple of logs on to keep it going while we fetched you."

"A couple of logs," Oswald said. "Look at that!"

Half-way up the slope of the hill a thornbush suddenly burst into flames. Then the wind freshened, and sparks began to fly over our heads.

"That's awkward," said Father, biting his lips.

A tuft of dry grass suddenly flickered into flame under his feet.

"Very," he added, jumping. "Here, we had better get back. I'll think up something to stop it as we go."

"Oh, you will, will you?" I snarled. "Well, you'd better think quick. It's all round this side already!"

The women set up a great clamour. The hill was almost encircled by a sea of fire, which was advancing rapidly to the top. The whole plain seemed to be alight, and a bright line of fire was moving steadily forward and lengthening every moment.

"There's a gap down there," cried Oswald, swinging a child on to his shoulder. "Grab the children and run for your lives!"

In a matter of seconds we were all racing downhill. We reached the gap before it closed, but down there the heat was ferocious and the noise deafening. The sun was obscured by a great pall of smoke. It was hard to breathe; harder still to see from which direction the fire was coming. Tongues of flame leapt out of the smoke first on one side and then on another. Little fires would burst out from underfoot; already our feet and legs were blistered.

"Make for the cave," shouted Father. "We shall be safe inside." Coughing and choking with the children squealing and writhing with pain and terror in our arms, we rushed on. But already we could see that our line of retreat was cut off; the fire could run faster than we could.

"It's no use, Father," shouted Oswald. "We can't get through. We must go the other way."

Father looked grim. There were no caves, no rivers, no firebreaks of any kind in the one direction which still lay open. If the fire had followed us there, we were cooked. But we had no choice now.

"Keep together!" shouted Father. "Oswald, you lead the way. I'll keep the women moving." He tore a stick from a bamboo thicket, and laid it smartly upon the behind of Petronella, who happened to be the last in our labouring, fugitive line. "Get on!" he shouted.

"I can't," she moaned. "I'm done."

"No you're not," Father roared. "Get *on*," and she staggered forward, until Alexander, already laden with two infants, came alongside and managed to give her an elbow to grasp. Then Father's stick fell unmercifully on the next straggler.

And now, to our amazement, we found we were not alone. Out of the undergrowth sprang bushbuck and antelope, zebra, impala and several warthogs and joined us, their eyes wide with terror. A small herd of giraffe bounded ahead of Oswald and served him well as scouts, but most of the game animals stayed with us, showing complete confidence in our leadership. I heard a heavy padding and panting by my side, and glancing round saw a young lioness with an almost newborn cub in her teeth. She dropped it at my feet, gave me a beseeching glance and bounded back to the flames, emerging a moment later with another cub in her teeth, but her fur singed. Taking first one of them a little way and then another, she kept up with us, and spared not a look at the gazelles whose sweating sides she brushed. She was joined a little farther on by a cheetah carrying a single cub, and soon after by a family of refugee baboons, their backs loaded with young. Finally there came a tremendous crash, and out of a giant euphorbia, whose top foliage had begun to smoulder, dropped Uncle Vanya.

"I told you so!" he bellowed furiously. "It's the end of the world! You've done it now, Edward!"

"Keep Mildred moving," Father replied. "You're only just in time!" And Uncle Vanya's entire energies were absorbed from that moment.

For a little while we seemed to gain on the fire. Right ahead of us was a rocky but low ravine, down which the whole company charged. We emerged into a wide expanse of grass and scrub; if the fire reached us there, it was the end. This now seemed certain, for both to right and left animals were racing towards us as though into an island of sanctuary. Even the snakes came hissing and terrified, rippling through the long grass. Only the birds, flying in dense formations, seemed to be safe; hawks, bustards and others among them profited by our disaster and dived on to snakes and small animals, carrying them off as easy prey. We were too exhausted to go forward; and then we saw it was useless to try, for the giraffes, who had galloped ahead once they reached the open country, now came cantering back. The ring had closed.

I climbed the rocks of the ravine, on which all sorts of animals lay and panted side by side, lion with buck, leopard with baboon, hyaena with antelope, all gazing with fascinated eyes at the blazing horizon. Two long horns of flame stretched far ahead, and clearly were going to meet if they had not already done so; worse still, the wind had veered slightly and the flames had begun to recoil on us. The way out of the ravine was blocked by the furnace of the burning forest; the way ahead was cut off by the flames racing towards us through the grass.

"It's no good!" I shouted to Father. "There's no way out, and it's beginning to come here."

"How long will it take to reach us?" shouted Father.

"Half an hour at most," I said.

"Come down, then, and help," shouted Father. When I joined them, he was issuing his orders in a sharp, incisive voice.

"Herd the children against the rocks. Then half of you follow Wilbur, and half me." He ran to one side, and Wilbur to the other.

I followed Father, and then to my horror saw that he had knelt down and was striking a stream of sparks from his flints into the tindery grass.

"Are you mad?" I screamed.

"We must make a firebreak of burnt grass which the main fire cannot cross!" he yelled back. "Wilbur and I will light it in small sections, then the rest of you take sticks and beat it out once the ground is bare. It's our only chance."

After a moment's thought, I saw the strategy of this, and began working like a driver-ant. In front of us, and moving down like a thousand red rhinoceroses, was the great curtain of flame and smoke. With what seemed hopeless slowness, we burned off the grass in small and bearable fires, beating and stamping them out as we worked, and slowly spread a black, fuel-less zone round our small sanctuary, crowded with women, children and shivering, terrified animals.

We had it ready just in time, and sprang back as great ravenous pillars of flame thundered down on us. A huge wave of scorching heat sent us reeling against the already oven-hot rocks. Frantically we tore up tufts of tussock grass and pressed them over the mouths and eyes of the children, while the animals squealed and writhed in agony as a monstrous cloud of smoke, thick with stinging particles of burning grass and twigs, blotted out everything.

But it passed. It passed round us and back towards the already blackened jungle from which it had come. Gradually the smoke cleared and it became easier to breathe. Then only one thought possessed us and the animals alike: to find water. Slowly the whole throng of us, two-legged or four-legged, stumbled through the hot ash and embers which were all that remained of the country, towards the nearest river. Nobody preyed on anybody else; each carrying or shepherding his own young, we staggered to the drinking places, where the crocodiles were waiting. But they were abashed by such a concourse of creatures; such a tremendous splashing of hoof and paw and foot they had never seen, and they sheered off. Then, with safety assured, thirst quenched and burns bathed, everybody looked at everybody else. In a flash the animals disappeared in all directions, except for one lost baby doe which nestled in William's arms.

"Well, there we are," said Father cheerfully. "You see what a wonderful invention it is. If we had not been able to make fire just when and where we wanted it, Wilbur and I, you'd all have been a mixed grill by now."

Uncle Vanya opened his mouth. Vainly he struggled to find words and then he closed it again, defeated. He rose, raised his hand to the sky in a gesture of despair, and lumbered slowly away, raising a choking cloud of white ash with every step. It was left to Griselda to comment. Black from head to foot, all her eyebrows and most of her hair burned off, she turned bloodshot eyes balefully on me.

"Your father," she croaked, "is *impossible*."

CHAPTER 18

It took us a long time to get back to the cave. Much of the country was still smouldering under the carpet of ash which covered it. We were in great pain from our burns and blisters; the children moaned and sobbed and had to be carried most of the way. Griselda's spirits were very low, but at last she had found Father out for the dangerous revolutionary that he was. I felt that this was something gained, and I tried to cheer her up by telling her of my important conclusions about the meaning of dreams: the brief visits to that other world which we make when the body is locked in sleep, and into which, it seemed reasonable to suppose, we slip entirely when finally we fall prey to somebody else. "Quite a philosopher, aren't you?" said Griselda, staring gloomily at her reflection in a pool which we happened to be passing. "Do you think the hair will grow again on this side, or will the rest come off and leave me bald for life?"

Everyone, in fact, was in a very bad temper except Father, who poked about in the ash with a stick with the utmost interest, and every now and then found roasted snakes, hyrax, squirrels and even duikers which he offered round saying it wasn't every day that we were given a hot meal free. We were in poor shape to enjoy the delicatessen, however. When we reached the cave, of course the fire was out. Father collected dried grass and leaves and some bits of charred wood from the burned forest, and got busy with his flint and ironstone and soon had another burning.

"There you are," he said proudly. "Maybe it was rather painful, but you see how well worth it! Fire when you want it, where you want it, with hardly more trouble than pressing a switch. It'll be a long time before they improve on this little gadget."

"Hm," said Oswald. "All the same, Father, it was hardly worth while your lighting the fire, seeing that we shall be moving almost at once."

"Moving! What on earth for?" exclaimed Father.

"Moving?" gasped Mother. "That's the first *I've* heard of it. And I hope the last."

"Moving?" cried Aunt Mildred. "I just couldn't. Not one step."

"Nevertheless," said Oswald, "we're moving. It seems to have escaped you all that Father's little experiments have burned up all the grass, to say nothing of most of the forest, for several hundred miles in every direction. No grass, I must observe, means no game. No game means no food. In short, we're practically on our way."

"Tomorrow to fresh woods and pastures new," I echoed mechanically.

"Tomorrow!" yelped the girls. "Oh, no, you can't mean it!"

"And that means," said Mother heavily, gazing at Father, "the end of the cave."

"I'll find you another cave, dear," said Father. "Er —this one *was* getting rather small for us, now the children have families of their own, don't you think? What we want," he went on, brightening up as he spoke, "is not just one cave, but a row of caves; semi-detached, as you might say. A limestone formation would be just the thing. What do you think, Wilbur?"

"Well, yes—" began Wilbur judicially, but Oswald cut in.

"What we want," he said, "is a nice tract of good hunting country. It's got to be good just because we have all got our families. So don't get any fancy ideas. Where the game lives, we live, whether there are limestone formations or what-have-you, or not. Hunting comes first."

"Oswald is right," said Griselda. "Meanwhile, however, in common with some of the other girls around here, I am shortly going to have a baby. How far away is this happy hunting-ground, Oswald dear?"

"I have not the least idea yet, you goose," said Oswald. "How should I? We shall just have to trek until we find it, that's all."

"How many days' trek?" insisted Griselda.

"I tell you I don't know. Ten, twenty, thirty, perhaps a hundred. So what?"

"And where am I going to have this baby?"

"Hang your baby! Have it in a bush and carry it on your back like a well-conducted female. And stop asking silly questions."

Clementina burst into tears. "Bub-bub-but Ossy

darling, I wanted so much to have ours *here*. It's so nice, what with the midden and the water and everything. I want to stay *here*."

"Shut up!" shouted Oswald. "You can't stay here, and that's that. Anyway, whose fault is it? I didn't burn off half the pasture in Uganda, did I?"

"I must say, Edward," Mother remarked, "that I do think you might have thought about the girls. Why, in their condition it's an absolute mercy that nothing dreadful has happened already. And now you want them to walk over hill and over dale—"

It was rare for Father and Mother to have words; in fact, I hardly ever saw him beat her; but at this he exploded. "Really, Millicent," he roared. "To listen to you, one would think that I neglected my family instead of working my fingers to the bone for the lot of you! Of course I think of the girls! Are you suggesting that making a fire with flints is no use to the girls? Or their children? Would you rather they went on in the old way, climbing a volcano every time they wanted to cook a duck for dinner? Is that your idea of pre-natal exercise? And what do you think would happen if the volcanoes became extinct, eh? Have any of you thought of that? I bet you haven't! Yes, I know they're big fires, but they'll burn out just like any *other*! Wilbur and I go to all this trouble—"

"I know, dear," said Mother. "But—"

"All this trouble," Father repeated. "And—er— think of the convenience of the thing—"

"Yes, dear, but the girls really aren't *fit* for a long journey."

"A long journey!" exclaimed Father. "Why there's absolutely nothing in a long journey now. In the old days, I admit, it was quite something. You got hunted by lions and chased by crocs, you couldn't find anything decent to eat, and you had to overnight in trees. But that's all over. Nowadays, wherever you stop, you just light a fire or two. That keeps the carnivores away. If it's wet, why, the fire dries you off in a brace of shakes! You can harden your speartips on safari. You can go after game with a spear in one hand and a burning brand in the other. You can—"

"Set the whole place on fire," I suggested.

"Fire *ad lib*," said Father, brushing this aside, "makes ours the dominant species once and for all. With fire and flint to world mastery, and our family in the forefront! Yet you talk about the girls! I am thinking about their children, who will be born into a better world than we dreamed of. I am building for the future, and you grumble about leaving your cave for a year or two—I suppose the confounded grass will grow again sometime? I look forward to the day when every horde will have its cave, every cave its fire, every fire its spit and every spit its roasting horse-flesh—when a journey will be a pleasant progress from one hospitable hearth to the next—"

But while Father was sentimentalizing about this possible palaeolithic arcady, I was thinking very quickly about the meaning of his words. I saw with contempt that Wilbur and Alexander and the women were falling for his sales-talk, and that even Oswald, usually so quick to spot the snags, had not seen the point. I waited for my chance, and then broke in hard and bitter.

"Do I understand, Father, that you propose to divulge this formula for fire-making to every Tom, Dick and Harry in Africa?"

Father stared at me. "Why, of course. What are you getting at?"

I paused for a moment before replying. Then, tightening my lips, I said quietly:

"Simply that I absolutely oppose any such unwarranted disclosure of horde secrets to unauthorized persons."

There was a deathly silence. The entire horde, I saw with satisfaction, was listening to me with startled attention. Father glanced round, and then said slowly:

"Oh, you do, do you? Suppose you tell us why."

"For quite a number of reasons," I said grimly, "which I hope the horde will find convincing. In the first place, because the secret is *our* secret—until *we* choose not to part with it. You have already thrown to the winds our once-for-all chance of a total monopoly of fire. I was too young to stop you from telling people how to get wild fire from volcanoes, and now, to judge by the smoke rising from the countryside, practically everybody, including my charming in-laws, has got it; and we are not one haunch of horse the better. Did you sell the secret? Did you license its use, Father? No, you did not! You gave it away, threw it away. Well, I am older now, and you are not going to throw the horde's property away this time, if I can help it."

"I see," said Father. "You propose to make them pay for a course of fire-making, do you? Six zebras for a lecture on how to hold the flint and laterite, six for one on the selection of dry tinder, six more for the final instruction on how to blow the smouldering into flame, eh? Is that what you have in mind?"

"I see nothing immoral in it," I said. "It would be dirt cheap at the price. But I don't suggest we should part with it at all yet. Artificial fire gives us an advantage worth far more than a few score zebra. People will have to admit that we are—well, dominant people. I don't think we should give that up. I am looking ahead. I am thinking that it might pay us best to be the only people who can make fire, and when other people want a fire started, well, they would have to send for one of us to make it for them—on terms, of course."

"Ernest!" shouted Father, purple with indignation, "I will not hear another word!"

"Oh, yes, you will," I said angrily. "You are not the only person concerned. I am thinking of the children! I am thinking of my sons' future careers, and Oswald's and Alexander's, yes, and of yours too, Wilbur! I really *am* thinking about the future of our children and not just romanticizing about it. And I say that we should not throw away the chance to set them up as professional fire-raisers and pyrotechnicians. I am not saying a word against hunting as a profession, Oswald; what I say is, there may be other professions, at any rate for the slower-footed amongst us."

"There's something in it," said Oswald. "After all, why should we give all these cads our ideas free, gratis and for nothing?"

"For the sake of the species, of course," said Father. "For subhumanity. To serve and to broaden the forces of evolution. To—"

"That's just a lot of words," I said brutally.

"Ernest!" cried Mother. "What can have come over you, to speak to your father like that?"

"I will speak to him as a son should to his father when he behaves as a father should to his son, Mother," I said quietly. "But ask yourself if he is doing so? Throwing away our chance to better ourselves for the sake of the species."

"Your father was always a very idealistic young man," Mother said, but I could see that she was shaken.

"I am a scientist," Father said quietly. "I consider that the results of research should be made available to subhumanity generally, to—well—to investigators of natural phenomena everywhere. In that way we shall all work together and build up a corpus of knowledge from which everybody will benefit."

"Of course, Dad," said Wilbur, and Father gave him a quick look of gratitude.

"I admire your principle, Father," I said. "I do, sincerely. But let me make two points about that. How much help have we ever received from any other investigators? I am morally certain that if there are any, they are sitting extremely tight on anything useful that they have found out. The only way to loosen them up will be to have something in reserve—something to trade with."

"There is that," muttered Wilbur unhappily, but Father sat rigid and unyielding.

"The other point," I went on, "is simply this. The discovery is still in an early stage. It has already led to one disaster. Even if we want to hand it out for the sake of the species, do we want to do so before it has been made safe? Safe for us and safe for them? Look how nearly we were all roasted. Only Father's brilliant inventiveness saved us in the nick of time—"

"I'm glad you noticed that," Father murmured.

"Would it be *kind*," I said slowly, "would it be *kind* to teach people who lack our know-how the way to fry themselves? And would it be sensible in everybody's interest to present to what are, after all, little more than apes, the means to burn up the entire country? One forest fire was bad enough—what would a score of them be like?"

Oswald slapped his thigh. "You're dead right!" he cried. "It's an appalling idea!"

I could see that I had Father isolated now. They were all on my side. Griselda gazed at me with shining eyes, and clapped vigorously. Even Mother said:

"I do think, Edward, that Ernest has given this a lot of thought. Don't you think, dear, we might just keep it to ourselves for a little while until we can see where we are?"

Father glared at her and got up. Then he stared at me, and I stared back.

"Hm," he said. "So that's the way you're going to play it, is it, Ernest?"

"That's the way I'm playing it," I said.

Father glowered at me for a moment; then he mastered his fury with an effort and his beetling brows went up at one corner in the old, humorous way.

"So be it, my son," he said.

He turned and marched into the cave, whither Mother followed him in a few minutes. I heard their voices in murmurous colloquy half the night.

CHAPTER 19

I wondered what Father's temper would be like next day in a mixture of exhilaration and dread. Would he be savage? Or would he have seen sense? He ought to be in a chastened mood, sulky, perhaps, but subdued. Whatever line he took, I was determined to hold my ground. I had challenged him, beaten him in argument and united his entire horde against him. He was clever, he was wily, he was powerful; but he had presumed on his authority and our respect. For once we were not going to submit to his irresponsibility or his bullying. I had made up my mind about that. In future, moreover, things were going to be different. Autocracy was done with; from now on big decisions would be made in family council.

Griselda was full of praise for the stand I had taken, and was active in rallying everyone to my side. She spent most of the night talking to the other women and enlarging on the risk to their children of permitting Father to let loose on an inflammable world the dangerous secret of fire-raising. She told me that they were, one and all, in favour of the very strictest control of it. "We'll keep it in the family," she said. "Petronella is talking to Wilbur. It's as much his idea as Father's. You know, Ernest, I've got an idea that Wilbur is just as clever as your father. But more amenable. He'll find a way to make it safe and then we'll go into business with it ourselves. I don't think we're as dependent on your father as you imagine."

But the next day Father was his usual sunny self, and to my surprise behaved as if the great family row had never taken place at all. He had a cheery word for everyone, briskly took charge of the preparations for the great trek to new hunting-grounds, and led the way with Oswald, carrying children pickaback in relays. Oswald decided the direction and Father set the pace, a slow one, to suit the women and children and the state of our scorched legs. He insisted that we should encamp early and chose the spot with care. He declared that it was unnecessary to make sure that there were nearby trees to climb—which was as well, since they were all badly burned. He made a circle of fires around our camp to test his belief that no animals would now attack us at night, even if we camped in the open. It was not altogether a fair test because the game had fled and most of its predators had followed it. Two or three pairs of bright eyes came up from a nearby swamp to have a look at us, and there was a good deal of disgusted grunting and sniffing, but whatever they were, they kept at a respectful distance.

We were hungry, for the land was burned bare and after the walk the women were too tired to search for food. We had to make do with kebabs of lizards and a few crocodiles' eggs. To keep us in heart Father cracked jokes and told the children stories. "Don't cry, darlings," he said, "and I'll tell you a story all about eating. Once upon a time there was a very big lion who was the finest hunter that had ever been known. He never failed to make his kill, and he could knock down any animal in the jungle, so swift was his spring, so terrible his claws. He loved hunting, too, and it was no trouble to him to make two or three kills a day. What annoyed him, however, was the way a lot of other people expected to cash in on his skill. He even grudged the other lions a share, but it made him absolutely furious when the hyaenas, jackals, vultures, and kites also turned up to help him eat his dinner—as well as ape-men, because this all happened in the days when we were scavengers too. "I have done all the work," growled the lion, "and these good-for-nothings expect to enjoy the results without making the slightest effort themselves. Why should I share with them? I won't." But his kills were so large and so frequent that he could not eat all the meat with which they provided him. No lion can. First of all he tried to kill the scavengers, but this only left him with an even bigger kill. The only way to keep his meat to himself, he saw, was to eat it all. So he tried. Even when he was completely full, he went on eating. He ate and ate and ate. He soon had frightful indigestion. Life became a perfect misery to him, he got horribly fat, but it gave him so much pleasure to see the baffled faces of the hyaenas and the ape-men that he went on with it, killing and eating for all he was worth. So, at quite an early age, he died, and being by then simply enormous, he gave just as good a meal to the hyaenas, vultures, jackals and ape-men as if he had shared his kill with them in the ordinary way."

"What did he die of?" asked the children.

"Fatty degeneration of the heart complicated by misanthropy," said Father, and crossing his hands over his empty stomach set an example to everyone by going peacefully to sleep.

During the journey he was particularly nice to Griselda and me. He took the opportunity to teach us how to make fire, and how to select the right stones to make the sparks fly plentifully. He said that a sound education was all he could hope to bequeath us when he died, and one never knew when one might step on a green mamba. "Make it your motto, my dears," he prosed, "to leave the world a little better than you found it, and give your children a bit better start than you had yourselves. Don't wait for the other fellow. Live as if the whole future of humanity depended on your efforts. After all, it may! These are critical times, very critical indeed. The mastery of fire is only a beginning. There must be thought, planning, organization if we are to build on this foundation. After natural science, social science! Who knows which of us may be privileged to discover how to harness the energies of ape-men more fully to the tasks of evolution, and be the first to lead us all to truly human ways? Think about it, my dears. I have the greatest confidence in you two. I doubt if I shall live to see it, but you may—that glorious golden age, that reward for all our struggles: to be human, to be *Homo sapiens* at last! I am getting on, you know, but I shall die happy if I can feel that my little efforts have done something to set you and yours on that road."

He bestowed on us the same humorous yet challenging look that he had given me after the family quarrel, and ambled away.

After a while Griselda said: "Ernest, we can say good-bye to the monopoly of fire-making. Father is going to chuck it to the winds as usual."

"He wouldn't dare," I exclaimed. "The horde is against it."

"Yes, he would," she said bitterly. "He thinks he knows what's good for the horde, better than the horde does. Oh, yes, he's going to sell us. He's been practically telling us. Didn't you realize? Daring us to try and stop him."

I thought hard. The harder I thought, the more it looked as if Griselda was right. Father's whole attitude, his cheerfulness, the silky, meaning way he talked, the sly digs at us, the pretended friendliness, added up to one thing: he had made up his mind to double-cross us and did not give a hang what we thought or did. If he had been furious; if he had rampaged and beaten us, we should have known that all was well, that he would abide by our ruling. But no; he meant to betray us.

"I don't see how we could stop him anyway," I said.

For a while Griselda said nothing, beyond the soft grunts she made from time to time as she felt the child stirring. She was very near her time, and walked very slowly. At last she said, "Ernest, do you really believe all that stuff about our going to that dream place when we are dead, that other hunting-ground which you say we visit in our sleep?"

"It's as good a hypothesis as any," I said. "We have got to go somewhere—our shadow, that is, has to."

"Our shadow?"

"A sort of inside shadow. It's there because when we're asleep it goes on all sorts of adventures. I told you."

"But," she said, "it's so odd, what we do when we dream. Not real."

"It feels real enough at the time," I said. "So it must be real. It's like the reflection of our bodies which we see in a pool; broken and wavy. But perhaps our bodies look as broken and insubstantial from that world. Something must happen to the inside shadow when the body is eaten up and becomes part of somebody else. Then what? Where does it go? We know only of that other, fragmentary hunting-ground, which we remember when we wake. It's reasonable to assume we go there. It's as good a hypothesis as any other."

"It's rather an important hypothesis in one way," said Griselda slowly.

"In what way?"

"It can't hurt anyone to—to send them there. They lose nothing much by it, if they get a mirror-body in the other hunting-grounds."

"No," I said. "Anyway, not if they have happy dreams, and not nightmares."

"Do you think Father has happy dreams?" Griselda asked casually. "Just for instance?"

My heart began to beat faster. But the answer needed no thought. It was obvious. All the images of Father—hunting, experimenting, bustling about—rushed together in my mind to frame it.

"Yes," I said. "Father has happy dreams, Griselda."

CHAPTER 20

The mighty bush-fire had burned itself out in a tract of barren country, where the earth was yet thin above the volcanic rock. Here we found no territory where the game could support so large a horde as ours had now become. I was possessed of a fine son, and so was Oswald, while Alexander doted on twin daughters. Wilbur was expecting to become a father any day. Aunt Mildred was also expecting; "It was all that music," she said happily, "and the way the girls were carried off. Vanya said that was the way to do things; that was the way things were done when he was a young ape, and, well, he took it into his head to knock me down and carry me into the bushes."

Father was delighted with the new babies, and examined their heads with tender fingers. "They're still small," he said. "But they're nice and soft, and they'll swell. You girls mustn't mind if having babies gives you more trouble as time goes on. There's no gain without pain. It's all evolution."

Day after day we struggled on, marching and hunting as we marched. At last we reached the top of a great range of tree-clad hills and found ourselves looking down on a rolling plain, intersected with glittering rivers, lakes that flashed in the sun, deep green swamps and thousands of square miles of hunting country, grass interspersed with woods and coverts and outcrops of rock; and beyond, again, another range of rocky hills.

"Game!" cried Oswald. "I can see it; I can smell it; I can almost hit it!" and he waved his spear in excitement.

"And there's the limestone and the caves," said Wilbur, pointing to the hills beyond.

"The promised land," I said.

Father smiled and said nothing, screwing up his

eyes to see against the glare of the declining sun. "Well, let's go down," he said at last, with a sudden sigh.

It was everything we expected; late as it was, we had prime roast venison, and plenty of it, for dinner that night. But I woke in the early dawn with a sense that something was wrong. I leapt up and saw that the others, too, were waking and groping round for the spears—which were not there. With a sinking heart I realized that we were half surrounded by a horde of strangers. They did not look at all friendly; they had our spears; and they outnumbered us. Then I perceived that Father was talking earnestly to an elderly ape-man who was evidently their horde-father.

"Parlez-vous français, Monsieur?" Father was saying ingratiatingly. *"Sprechen-Sie Deutsch, mein Herr? Habla español, Señor? Kia ap hindi bol secte ho? Aut latina aut graeca lingua loquimini?* Of course you don't—what am I thinking of. Back to the old sign language," he went on, as the other shook his head at every question.

It was a slow business, as they alternately pointed to trees, grass, spears, sons, the bones of the buck we had eaten the previous evening, and each other's bellies. However, they seemed to be making steady progress by the afternoon, and the tension had greatly relaxed. By nightfall they were getting almost cordial, and we were brought a small quantity of food to eat—raw, however. We had not kept up the fire, but now, watched by the strangers with the greatest of interest, we blew up the embers and managed to cook the small fare they had brought—a few hyrax, a bush-baby and a large tortoise. Father induced their leader to try a few morsels of this last, and judging by the rolling of his eyes, he appreciated it.

"Well," Father said, as the strangers finally withdrew some distance, carefully taking our spears with them, "I'm sorry it has taken so long, but that's the trouble with any universal language—slow, repetitive and lacking in subtlety. The situation is quite simple, however, and boils down to this. Trespassers will be prosecuted."

"You mean they've bagged this whole plain?" gasped Oswald. "Well, of all the nerve!"

"He says they don't make anything wonderful of it," said Father. "They have not got our advanced hunting techniques, you know. And, like us, they've got big families. They say we've got to move on. Or else."

"It seems absurd," I said. "There's plenty of room

for everybody. Anyway," I added, "I dare say it's 'or else,' whatever we do, if they're as hungry as all that."

"Relations have not been broken off yet," said Father. "Negotiations will be resumed tomorrow. It is not too late to hope that a formula can yet be reached, satisfactory to both parties. I intend, on your behalf, and mindful of the grave issues at stake, to explore every avenue. Meanwhile, I fear, we must regard ourselves as on our honour not to try to escape. Sentries have been posted."

"Dirty wogs," growled Oswald. We composed ourselves to sleep in no very cheerful state of mind.

The next day was a repetition of the preceding one. The two plenipotentiaries squatted apart, gesticulating with their arms and occasionally jumping up and miming some operation such as flint-chipping or cutting somebody's throat; the rest of us sat glumly round the ashes of our fire, since we were not allowed to stray and gather fuel. Oswald had tried to get himself a club under this pretext, but had been driven back at spear-point. "Dirty wogs," he said; this had quickly become his favourite expression.

We got little food that day; but Father returned from the conference at sundown distinctly more hopeful. "There's a chance," he said. "Quite a chance. I am not pessimistic."

"Are they going to let us stay, then?" I inquired.

"A full communiqué will be issued when the talks are over," Father said, rather pompously in my opinion. "Meanwhile, you must not expect me to make any statement that might be premature."

On the following day, however, it became clear that agreement was in sight. The two horde-fathers, in fact, seemed to be on the best of terms, laughing, joking, and slapping each other on the back. Finally they rose and disappeared into the bush together. We became extremely anxious as time passed and they did not reappear. Hours went by, but still there was no sign of them, and I suspected foul play. But there was nothing we could do about it, weak with hunger and surrounded by our well-armed and well-fed captors.

Then my heart missed a beat. Smoke could be seen spiralling up beyond the trees.

Sick at heart, we waited for the inevitable end.

Then suddenly we saw Father walking briskly towards us, alone.

"It's all right," he said. "I've fixed everything up. The heads of agreement have been—er—initialled, and the treaty will be ratified at a grand feast tomorrow at which, my dear," he turned to Mother, "you will greatly oblige me if you make a really special effort with your famous *tortue rôtie en carapace à la bohémienne*. It has been my lifeline all through these difficult discussions, and I really don't know that I could have pulled things off without it."

"Yes, but what is the agreement?" I demanded.

"Head One," said Father impressively. "We are to have half the plain to hunt in, and provision is made for a boundary delimitation commission to be constituted hereinafter."

"Half? Well done," said Oswald.

"Head Two," Father went on. "Neither horde is to poach in the territory of the other. Head Three: we are to have the mountainous bit at the western end."

"That's got all the limestone caves," said Wilbur. "What made them part with it?"

"It's full of cave bears," said Father happily. "He seemed most anxious we should have it. They've got some small rock shelters high up on a cliff only a few miles away, and even so they're always having their babies pinched by leopards. Of course, he doesn't know we can deal with bears."

"Smart work," I said approvingly.

"Not bad," said Father. "Actually, he thinks he's put a very fast one across us. Head Four: the hordes shall be friends, shall have freedom to evolve in their own way, shall intermarry exogamously and shall work together to achieve peace, progress and prosperity. There! One always ends these things with a bit of rodomontade, you know."

"And what about Head Five?" asked Griselda sharply. "Or is that a secret covenant?"

"Head Five?" asked Father. "What do you mean?"

"Head Five," retorted Griselda. "The one that runs in consideration of all of which the horde that knows how to make fire hands over the secret to the horde that doesn't."

"That isn't actually in the treaty," said Father. "But it was only fair—"

That telltale spiral of smoke! And we had been fools enough to think Father in danger!

"You've told them how to make fire!" I cried. "Without asking us. No wonder you got a fine agreement. You—You—"

"I know I didn't consult you, my boy," said Father quietly. "But you must see that we were in a pretty sticky position. I had to trade something, and I was lucky to have that to trade."

"I don't believe it," I raved. "You didn't have to

give them that. Now they're as good as us! Besides, you'd have given it to them anyway, you know you would. You *wanted* to give it."

"I had to give it," said Father.

"How do we know that?" Griselda hissed. "How do we know that there was any real danger? You must have cooked up the whole thing—or most of it, anyway."

Father shrugged his shoulders.

"It's all absurd, you know. You can't suppress these things. Fire will be the commonplace of the next generation. What we have to think about is something else, something new that *won't* be a commonplace. That's the way to get on."

"You have thrown away our birthright," I said. "You have put a deadly weapon in the hands of a primitive people. You—"

"I suppose they *will* be safe with it?" Mother asked.

"Perfectly safe," Father said gravely. "I gave the most detailed instructions for use. On terms, of course. The best hunting in Africa. Let's hunt now, shall we? I'm famished."

CHAPTER 21

F ather had outsmarted us again. There was nothing we could do about it. The hunting was excellent and the caves were everything we could wish —we took a complete terrace of them, with a sunny northerly aspect. But it was galling to see our neighbours, who had been mere canaille, making fires all over the place, and popping over repeatedly to swap recipes for *côte d'antelope à la manière du chef,* or asking us to join them in a barbecue. Father declared that they were very nice people, and when, inevitably, they did burn off most of their pasture, waved it away with a cheerful "mistakes will happen in the best-regulated families," and insisted on presenting them with a year's licence to hunt on our side of the boundary-line. From first to last he never had the faintest notion of what was due to people with our position to keep up.

Griselda was extremely bitter about it. She convinced herself that the trouble with the reception committee on our arrival had been a completely put-up job. "I know your father, how he manages things," she said darkly, and, remembering what happened to Elsie, I believed her. She added that even if we had been in some danger, Father had gone the wrong way about getting round it. "We should have shown what wizards we were with fire," she said, "and then they would have been too frightened to attack us, the miserable savages. We should have established our moral supremacy, and that would have solved the servant problem, too. I wouldn't have to do every blessed thing myself in this cave if those beastly girls from over the way had to come to me every time they wanted a chump chop." Again and again she warned me to keep a sharp eye on Father. "He'll do it again," she said. "Mark my words. The old man is becoming a positive danger to the horde."

I thought this was putting it a bit strongly, but in the end I had to admit she was right.

Soon after we had settled down in our new homes, Father resumed his experiments. For a very long time nothing came of them, nor would he disclose what he was after. More immediately exciting developments claimed our attention. Wilbur was building up a large-scale palaeolithic tool manufactory; he had dozens of skilled operatives working under him, but even so, his ovate hand-axes were in such demand throughout Africa, that he found it hard to fulfill all his orders. Alexander, too, was developing interior cave-decoration in a very big way with a whole range of new ochreous pigments. I contended that his murals were even better for the hunting than the new bolas with which we tripped up the game and the horn-tipped spears with which we dispatched it. Success continued to elude William's efforts to evolve the hunting-dog, admittedly; but his attempts at least enlivened our daily routine. "It's the dog or nothing," he would insist, as we bound his bleeding limbs in arum leaves. "And kindness with firmness is the answer. It must be." We could not persuade him that the idea was chimaerical. More practicable was Mother's invention of the zebra-skin hand-bag. There was also a great deal of fuss over the way the women had begun to make a habit of wearing the hides of animals, and rushing in and out of each other's caves with screams of "My dear, look at this! It's the very latest!" or wails of "My lovely leopard has gone as hard as a board, darling, and just look at the way the fur comes out of this monkey. What can I do for it?" Griselda was the leader in all this nonsense, to which Oswald and I took strong exception; needless to say, our views made not the slightest difference. "Don't be an old Vanya" was the invariable retort to every protest. But we could see exactly where such decadent frivolity would lead. Now, of course, every young fop must needs support his fig-leaf.

So time passed, until one day Father came to me and said, "I've got something to show you, my boy," and I immediately knew from the suppressed triumph in his voice that we were in for really serious trouble. I followed him a considerable distance into the forest, until we reached a glade. "My little workshop," said Father, waving his hand with modest pride. Neat little stacks of broken pieces of wood, each from three to five feet long, all carefully labelled with leaves of different trees, were disposed in orderly rows. "It's been a big job," said Father. "I began, as you see, with camphor here, and went on with olive, yellow-wood, pinkwood, stinkwood, sandalwood, pillar-wood, greenheart and smokeyheart. I even tried ebony, mahogany and teak. I began, of course, with bamboo; but apart from giving me the basic idea, it's hopeless stuff. It may have a future in building, but I simply detest it myself. I tried fig, the ironwoods, chestnut and even acacia; but it wasn't until I reached yew that I felt I had something of real promise. After that I concentrated on yew; all these broken bits are yew. When it's too green it has no elasticity, and when it's dead it breaks. You must get it absolutely right; and it improves with seasoning, though I'm only at the very beginning there. Here you have my ideas for strings; I've tried everything I can think of, and the leg tendons of elephant come up best, with the rootlets of the vanilla orchid a close runner-up. For your shafts, any good, straight light wood will do —such as sandalwood. Avoid the heavies, they have penetrative qualities, but unduly reduce the range."

"What are you talking about?" I asked, after this had gone on for some time.

"Archery," said Father simply. "I know it's a bit before its time, really, but I just had to have a stab at it. Wilbur has fixed you up with bolas, I know, and I dare say Oswald will stumble on the boomerang principle when his legs get varicose veins like mine. This, however, is the ultimate weapon. Like to see?"

And there and then Father picked up the first bow ever made. Mark I was a clumsy, four-foot affair, bent more at one end than at the middle, with several unscraped lumps in it, and a string that stretched atrociously. Yet it drew! To it he fitted a prototype arrow, bent the bow and let fly. The projectile shot forth and fell to the ground over thirty yards away. "I can do much better than that," said Father, enjoying my astonishment. "This string is always getting slack. You have a go."

After several false starts, I fired an arrow twenty-five yards.

"Well, what do you think of it?" said Father. "Remember, this is only a mock-up job."

"The possibilities are stupendous, Father," I said sombrely. I looked at the old man sadly. This was the end. The absolute end.

"We'll have a grand feast to celebrate this," Father said.

"We will," I said heavily.

"I meant to show it to Oswald first," Father went on, "as it's more in his department than yours, but he's off hunting today, as you know, and I simply had to show someone."

"I'll tell Oswald," I said. And I did. Griselda too.

It was quite evident what we had to do. It did not take more than one demonstration of the bow and arrow to convince Oswald. He was by far the greatest hunter for miles around, outrunning and outranging everybody else. "When everybody has one of these, Oswald," was all I had to say, "you'll be just as good a hunter and marksman as the next fellow. No better, no worse. Strength and skill won't matter any more."

"It'll be the end of all true skill and all true sport if every tenth-rate rotter can have a bow and a bag of arrows to shoot big game," said Oswald. "What on earth possessed Father to— Well, what are we going to do about it?"

"I am afraid that whatever we do will have to be done quickly," I said. "Remember about fire?"

"Holy Megatheriums! It's too dreadful to contemplate! You must think of something, Ernest."

"I have," I said.

"Well, what is it?"

"At the next test-firing," I said, "there will have to be an accident."

Oswald went very white. "You can't mean that."

"Have you any better idea?"

"But—"

"I know," I said. "I know. But he's an old man

now. He hasn't got much longer anyway. He ought to have retired long before this, but you know what he is. I think, Oswald, it's kinder this way. He'll be far better off in the happy hunting-grounds. Let him play with bows and arrows there! It'll be a bit of a shock to them, I dare say. But it'll be no loss to him —the remaining years ahead of him in the non-dream world. His varicose veins are terrible, you know."

"I know your theories," Oswald said, slowly. "We don't die. We pass on. That helps with this—this painful duty. I don't like it, but I'm afraid you're right. We must protect the public."

"Well said, Oswald," I said warmly. My brother was coming on well, as the passing years endowed him with responsibility and experience.

"I will arrange everything," I added.

"Then we can suppress this filthy thing," Oswald said, nodding.

"Let's say—keep it on the secret list," I replied easily.

Oswald suggested a few trifling improvements to the weapon—I forget what exactly, something to do with putting feathers on the ammunition, I think. Father was extremely pleased. "Invention is team work," he declared. The first tests went off successfully, but then my turn came, something went wrong

with the arrow—the feathers came off or the shaft
was bent—and Father had foolishly run in front to
pick up his own arrow. He fell without a murmur.

It seemed odd that Father couldn't make a speech at
the end of the feast. But I felt sure that he would have
wished me to say a few words, and I did. About the
duty of devoting ourselves to becoming truly human,
the example he had set us all, and the need to temper
progress with forethought. I could sense him within
me, shaping the phrases and suggesting the conclusions. I sat down amid applause, and poor Mother
was in floods of tears. "It sounded *exactly* like your
poor, dear father," she said. "I only hope you will be
a little more careful than he was, though."

So that was the end of Father in the flesh, my son,
and the end he would have wished himself—to fall
by a really modern weapon and to be eaten in a really
civilized way. We thus ensured his survival, both
body and shadow. He lives on within us, while his
inside shadow is making mincemeat of the dream-
elephants in the hunting-grounds of the other world.
I am not at all surprised that you have met him there
once or twice, or that you were so much impressed
when you did. But, as you see, he had his kindly side.

He was, we like to think, the greatest ape-man of the Pleistocene—and that is saying something. I have told you this story, that you may know how much indebted to him we all are for the comforts and conveniences with which we are surrounded. His was perhaps rather a practical rather than a speculative bent, but let us not forget his unflinching faith in the future, and let us remember, too, that in his passing he helped to shape the basic social institutions of parricide and patriphagy which give continuity both to the community and to the individual. Indeed, indeed, he was the mightiest tree in the forest, and you do well to think of him when you pass it. Perhaps he will think of you.

But he did not actually make the whole world, no. Who did make it? I am afraid that is quite a different question, which I cannot go into now. For one thing, it is very complicated, even controversial. And for another, it is long past your bedtime.

THE END OF THE PLEISTOCENE